THE INDENTED HEAD

R.K. Wilson

For Gabriel

"To see a World in a Grain of Sand
And a Heaven in a Wild Flower
Hold Infinity in the palm of your hand
And Eternity in an hour"

William Blake, Auguries of Innocence

The List

Prologue

I'd tailgate traumatising tales of extraterrestrials, lizard men and greys; interplanetary beings who piloted the psyches of politicians and world leaders. I'd dragnet dastardly deeds done in paranormal pizza parlours. I went to places where lunatics lampooned lunar landings and talked of nine-foot Neanderthals nesting in the Antarctic. There were posts about Dionysian devotees dancing in Bohemian woods. It was a place where Satan's servants sacrificed their sanity and wars were preplanned, where the harpies of HARP warped the weather, and control freaks fraternised with fate and fertility, pathologising population control.

"Jesse! Jesse!" I heard my mother calling. Her voice seemed a long way away. "Hurry up, I need help packing the car! I need you here on planet earth! Will you get out of that snake hole!"

I clawed my way to the surface, gasping for air. I heard my disembodied voice say, "Rabbit; rabbit hole."

"I don't care what kind of hole it is! Just get out of there and get packing! Or *get packing*!"

She always spoke to me as if I were a naughty nine-year old. She failed to notice that I had grown up. "You don't want to end up like one of those basement dwellers, do you?"

"We don't have a basement," I reminded her.

"Don't try to be smart, I need you to give me a hand."

I finished my post and shut down. My head ached, my eyes were blurry; it had been a long night.

It was Boxing Day and we were doing what we always did; leaving the real world and going to that retro-utopia, that parallel universe where nothing bad ever happened.

Demented Head

Indented Head, my mother said, wasn't so much a geographical location as a state of mind. Either way, that was where we went every summer. As far back as I can remember we spent every summer at Indented Head.

Everyone who camped there seemed to have a different story about how the place got its name. Most people thought it had to do with the shape of the bay, which looks something like a head with a dent in it. Others believed the unlikely story that it went all the way back to the First World War, when an Aussie soldier was shot in the chest, but the bullet didn't penetrate because he'd had a coin in his pocket. Instead of putting a dent in his chest, it put a dent in King George's head. When the soldier got back to Oz and built his house on the bay, he took out his coin, stared at it long and hard, thought about the war and wondered why he had survived when so many others had died. So, as a tribute to King George, who had inadvertently saved his life, he called the place Indented Head and the name just stuck.

Then there were those who believed that the name was inspired by the wreck of the Ozone; a great paddle-steamer sunk in the sands off shore, with one mighty paddle wheel protruding above the water-line like a giant head, and in the spaces between the paddles, people imagined great translucent eyes that gazed at the campers on shore. The wreck wasn't just a place to hang out, it was the iconic symbol of the place, the spiritual heart of the place; the place where campers laid their bodies and their souls. That giant wheel was the equivalent of the cross to Christians or the Wheel of Dharma to Buddhists. But above all, it was our place.

Sometimes when I looked around the caravan park, it seemed like everyone had an 'indented head' one way or another. People would sit for hours in front of their caravans, dead still, semi-comatose, staring out to sea, watching the shifting streams of green; every shade from the deepest olive through to the palest apple. And there, bobbing gently on the horizon like a faded Fata Morgana, was Melbourne; the lost city of far away and long ago, forgotten in the pressing immediacy of green seas, synthetic sun shades and snorkelling under the wreck.

For me, Indented Head was defined by three iconic land marks; the empty caravan high on a cliff to the North, the wreck of the Ozone way out in the water to the East and our dilapidated caravan the 'Costa de Plenty' sitting on a beachfront site to the South, and right slap bang in the middle of these three points was where we used to light our camp fire at night. It was sort of like the Bermuda Triangle, a vortex to other worlds or maybe a place from which we could see this world more clearly.

I guess there's a defining year, or a defining summer in everyone's life. For me, it was the year I graduated from High School. It was the summer we solved the mystery of the empty caravan, the summer I fell in love, the summer my parents split up and the summer I felt like I had betrayed my best friend. It was also the summer I finally understood the meaning of the saying "The whole is greater than the sum of its parts."

Mum

It struck me that my mother's head was more, 'indented' than most. When visitors came, she'd point to the sign emblazoned on the front of our caravan 'Costa de Plenty.' She would roar with laughter and say, "It costa de nothing!" which was true.

One morning, after a stormy night, when our tent had collapsed on top of us for the tenth time, a second cousin twice removed drove past dragging an old rust-bucket behind him, on the way to the tip. He'd just dropped by to invite us to dinner. Mum looked at that decrepit excuse for a caravan as if it were Buckingham Palace on wheels. It was love at first sight and she just had to have it. So, instead of spending its last years disintegrating at the tip, it was loaded onto our camp site and became the hub of happy summers for years to come.

'Costa de Plenty!' Maybe the bay had been the Coast of Plenty when that caravan's first owners had camped on the bay, but things had changed since then. Campers who went out in their boats sometimes came back empty handed, complaining that the fish were undersized and that the bay had been fished out. There used to be hundreds of varieties of fish, but years later there were just a few flatheads, or garfish, or the odd squid. Fishermen complained that the big netters were taking more than their fair share, and we all noticed that the crabs were disappearing, either because people were taking too many, or because the habitat was changing.

When I was a little kid, we'd spend hours crabbing. We'd lift rocks and watch the crabs scuttle away, evading our grasping fingers and disappearing among the velvety green tendrils of sea weed, deep in the glinting rock pools. We used to catch big red crabs the size of a man's hand, and strange white ones with the most intricate patterns on their shells. There were green ones marked with ancient hieroglyphs and tiny grey ones, each with its own imprint. Just like fingerprints, we never found any two shells the same. Years later we could barely find a single tiny grey.

On still nights when the tide was out, we'd creep sure footed through the shallows, spear guns poised above our heads. We'd poke stingrays out of our path, side step sea snakes and every now and then spear a banjo shark. One year I speared my friend Aaron's foot. His parents had to drive him into Geelong hospital late at night to get it out. He was crying and swearing the whole way, telling me he hated my guts and that he'd never fish with me again, at least not at night. He limped through the rest of that summer and kept his distance whenever I had a speargun in my hand.

But the year I want to talk about was the year of rebellion; the year I finished High School. My mother had worked hard at 'tutoring' me, with a daily tirade of encouragement to make sure I would get into a good university, and she was so proud when I finally graduated high school and enrolled in her favourite university to study her two favourite subjects; literature and politics. Then, she was so angry when I told her that I wasn't going to go, that I didn't want to do literature and politics, that they were subjects for dickheads and dropkicks and that I wasn't *her*, and that I wanted to become a brickie. Her eyes flashed a nasty shade of red and she started to shake. Her upper lip curled and smoke swirled from her nostrils. She hissed something inaudible. Then with a mighty shriek, the tirade began:

"A brickie! A friggin' brickie! I worked my fingers to the bone to turn you into an intellectual, a writer, the writer you claimed you wanted to be when you were six! Six! If you wanted to rebel, why didn't you just get drunk and join a rock and roll band?"

"Mum, people don't do that anymore" I protested.

"What? What do they do? Become brickies?"

She kept spitting out the word 'brickie' like she had eaten a mouldy lump of cheese.

"It's a waste of an intellect! A waste of a good mind!"

It wasn't my mind I was worried about; it was my grandmother's mind. She had developed Alzheimer's and had come to live with us. It was strange to watch a mind detach itself from its intellectual anchor and wander aimlessly in the eccentric orbit of a parallel universe. She mistook the cat for the dog and tied an electric cord around its neck and took it for a walk around the block. She confused the toilet with the washing machine. She collected all the dirty undies and socks and flushed them down with a liberal cup of laundry detergent. When Mum tried to rescue a sock, she stuck a stick down the toilet and hauled out a brown one, waving it in the air like a triumphant flag. In a moment of clarity Nan screamed "What are you doing?"

"Getting this out of the loo!" growled Mum.

"Are you mad?" shouted Nan, "Poo should be left in the loo!" She tried to wrestle the stick from Mum and in the tussle the sock flew off the stick and landed on Nan's head. She stood there screaming "Get it off! Get it off!" until Mum pulled it off and flushed it down the toilet. Looking at me, Nan said, "Your mother's not right in the head! She can't tell the difference between the washing machine and the loo!"

Mum thought about taking Nan camping with us that summer, but decided it might be better to put her into respite care until we got back.

The Christmas Party

The two most important dates on Mum's social calendar were Kid's Christmas and The Indented Head Fancy Dress.

Every Christmas Mum would invite the parents and kids, that I had met in kinder and prep, over to our house for dinner. She'd set up two big tables with red table cloths and miniature mechanical, all-singing-all dancing Christmas trees, and lay out nuts and dried fruit, and bowls of big fresh cherries. She'd hang red and white elf hats on the back of each chair and insist that everyone put on a hat as soon as they arrived, so that we looked like a pack of laughing lunatics.

After we'd polished off the prawns and salmon and roast turkey and potato salad and pavlova, we'd all go and sit in front of the Christmas tree that she'd painstakingly decorated. She'd always choose the biggest tree and when the shop owner delivered it, my father would snarl at him, as if he were personally responsible for making the next two hours of my father's life pure hell. The man would dump the tree on the lounge-room floor and head out the front door as fast as his chubby legs would carry him. He'd always pause at the front gate and listen, just to make sure that the yearly argument had begun, then he'd grin and wink at me and say, "It's going to be another Merry Christmas." Then he'd jump into his van and drive off to finish his deliveries.

Mum would start, "It's not going to fit in the bucket!"

"It'll fit! I'll make it fit!" shouted Dad.

"You're going to chop off the bottom branches!" Mum would accuse him.

"How else can I make it fit?"

"It will spoil the shape."

"You have to sacrifice something!"

"Not the shape! I got one with a perfect shape!"

"Then you do it! You put the stupid thing in the damn bucket! There's no trunk on it. You never get one vith a trunk!" Dad would yell, totally frustrated. My German father never pronounced his 'Ws.'

"Alright, just do what you want, but it's going to look too short. Who wants a short Christmas tree?" cried Mum.

"Me! I vont a short Christmas tree, a tiny Christmas tree, a non-existent Christmas tree! Vhy do we have to have a real Christmas tree? Vhy can't we just get an artificial tree like everyone else?" Dad would raise the quintessential question.

"Because artificial Christmas trees are not real! And the whole point of Christmas is to have a real tree!" Mum would counter.

"That's not the whole point of Christmas! I can't see the point of Christmas! Vot is the point of Christmas?" Dad's question cut to the core.

"The point of Christmas is to give thanks for all the good things in our lives, like friends and family and most of all, kids!"

"Then get the kid to put the tree in the bucket, or better still put the kid in the bucket and decorate him!" Dad would scream.

"Jesse, Jesse come help your dad put the tree in the bucket!" Mum would beg me.

I would slide under the bed, which got harder as I grew older, and I would pray to Santa to hurry up and make Christmas end, so that we could get down to Indented Head.

But to get back to the Christmas dinner, we'd all sit around the Christmas tree and the ritual would begin: First the Kriss Kringle, where one person would go to the tree and pick up a present marked a mum, a dad, or a kid and give it to someone in the circle. Then that person would choose the next present and so on until all twenty-five of us had a present. Then Mum would pass around the Christmas cups filled with lollies and chocolates. She'd keep handing out the cups and we'd pass them on around the circle, sweltering in the heat while the song 'I'm Dreaming of a White Christmas' droned on and on in the background. Then later as darkness fell, Mum would stage the Xmas Puppet Show.

When I was about four, Dad built a portable puppet theatre with three folding partitions and an ornate window perched on top, with two red velvet curtains which could open and close at the pull of a string. Over the years I'd painted the partitions with strange kid images of Christmas trees and Santa hanging on a cross and snowmen. And right in the centre, I'd painted the big paddle wheel of the wreck of the Ozone with Christmas presents dangling off it, because the wreck was the best present my parents ever gave me.

Mum's annual puppet show was usually about the three wise men getting lost in the desert and forgetting to bring the gold, the myrrh and the frankincense. The show always ended with the same line from one of the wise puppets; 'I may have forgotten the frankincense but I've brought the gift of common sense.'

The three wise men were Gab from Ireland, Bill from Australia and Kamal from India, and the narrator was a tiny pink pig. My job was to shine a big torch at the curtains and hold my hand steady for the whole show. Mum would bob down behind the partitions, quickly switching accents and puppets as she played all the characters and attempted to reconcile the Jesus story with her own crazy beliefs. She never could understand why the Three Wise Men didn't bring the baby Jesus gifts of real wisdom rather than just gold and expensive incense. She'd say, "The story doesn't make sense! Those wise men just brought money! Myrrh was worth more than gold, and frankincense was worth more

than myrrh and gold put together! What happened to
all the money? How come the kid ended up so poor?
My mother would stare at me expecting some sort of
response. I felt theologically ill-equipped to answer
her questions. I used to shrug my shoulders and say, "I
dunno, maybe his parents spent it before he grew up."

Mum would always begin the show in a squeaky voice,
the voice of Piggy the narrator:

Let me tell you a story that spans from now 'til way
    back then
'tis the story of Jesus and the Three Wise Men
But there's a mystery to this history
What happened to the Frankincense, Myrrh and
    Gold?
It disappeared, so I'm told
Some say his parents used it for their own pleasure!
Others say the Wisemen turned it into buried
    treasure

To begin, it was old Joseph's and young Mary's
    wedding night
And they had both agreed not to fight
As Mary lay on the wedding bed, a wet towel draped
    across her head
That was when old Joseph said
I think I need to take a pee
I'll just nick out to the lemon tree
When he was gone, Mary opened her eyes
And then she got a lovely surprise
There stood a boy with big white wings
He wasn't wearing any other things

He whispered, I've been sent by God to do a very
    special job
He's even given me a brand new nob
Now open your legs and close your eyes
And I'll try and bring it up to size
Then he entered with God's mighty member
And gave Mary a moment she'd always remember
When the deed was done he kissed her cheek
And said he wished he could come back in a week
Then in a flash the boy was gone
Leaving Mary feeling quite forlorn
When old Joseph returned she tried to explain
But as he listened he thought her quite insane
Well nine months later the baby Jesus was born
Which filled King Herod's heart with scorn

Then, Mum would slip her hand into the red devil
puppet and put on a posh English accent to play King
Herod:
My name is Herod I am King of this land
I can sing, I can dance, I can do a handstand
I can dance, I can sing, I can do anything
I'm even partial to a romantic fling
I'm a very happy chappy
Especially when I'm dancing in my nappy
But of late I confess I've been feeling sad
My advisor told me something bad
He said that a new king had been born
You can imagine how my heart was torn
A new King says I
Are you off your nut?
Where is he? In some peasant's hut?

Rumour has it sire he's a virgin birth
Well the entire court filled with mirth
What you mean she done it all on her own?
With a bit of help from God's almighty bone
Well go chop off his little head
Just make the little bastard dead
But sire, I'm not sure he can be found
Then for heaven's sake send out the hounds
Sire hundreds of babies have been born this year
Then I'll have all their heads don't you fear
But sire I'm not sure it can be done
Rubbish! Let's have some bloody fun

Then Piggy, the narrator puppet would come back and
say:
But as you know the baby Jesus was out of danger
As he lay fast asleep in his little manger
Some say he lay there in disguise
As he waited for the three men wise

Then the play would cut to the three wise men, with
Mum slipping her hands in and out of puppets and
swiftly changing accents. Wiseman Gab was a green
alligator puppet with an Irish accent:
Lately I've been talking to God
And you know he told me something odd
He said I was to bring his son some gold
And that I was to do just what I'm told
So I asked my wife for a few pennies
But she shrugged and said she hadn't any
So here I am in a foreign land
Knee deep in desert sand

And nought that's nothing in my hand
But from Ireland I bring the gift of the gab
The gift of the blabberty blabberty blab
Every year I kiss the Blarney Stone
Then give a speech in impeccable tone
We Irish understand the gift of the word
And that the pen is mightier than the sword
But it was meant to be wisemen three
Not just I, myself and me
Oh where oh where is wiseman Bill?
He was meant to meet me on this hill

Then, Mum would quickly switch to a football player
puppet and put on a broad Aussie accent:
G'day. How are ya? Me name is Bill
And I'm looking for a bloody hill
And I'm looking for a new born babe
The one that God almighty made
I'm supposed to bring him a little gift
To give the lad a bit of a lift
But the truth is I feel like a bloody cur
'Cos I forgot to bring the bloody myrrh
So the gift I bring is a gift from down under
'Tis the knowledge to avoid a nasty chunder
My wisdom relates to the raw prawn
Make sure it's cooked through or ya could throw up
   on the lawn
And while we're at it
Make sure you've got plenty of mates
'Cos a lonely heart can fill with hate
But we're supposed to be wisemen three
Not just I, myself and me

So where the hell is wiseman Kamal?
Hope he didn't take a wrong turn at the Taj Mahal

Then Mum would change over to a monkey puppet with
an Indian accent:
Golly gosh I seem to be lost
What the price? What the cost?
Yes my name is Kamal and I hail from the East
The land of wisdom where Karma is beast
What is Karma you may well ask
It is the wisdom of being taken to task
Do unto others as you would have them do unto you
Keep a heart that's good and true
Oh just be good for goodness-sake
Or you could come back as a lizard or a snake
But wisdom is not what I was meant to bring
I was meant to bring that other thing
That thing they call sweet frankincense
But far better is the gift of common sense
Oh but it's meant to be wise men three
Not just I, myself and me!
Where oh where could the others be?

Finally, Mum would put the tiny piggy puppet on her
finger again and in a squeaky voice finish the show:
Well finally the three men found each other
In knowledge and wisdom they were indeed brothers
And once they knew they were out of danger
They made their way to that special manger

So you see the baby Jesus was meant to grow up
    wealthy
But instead, he grew up poor but healthy!

Well now all good stories must come to an end
And so another year passes with you my dear
      friends.

Then Mum would crawl out from behind the puppet
theatre and take a bow, and I'd breathe a sigh of relief
knowing that we'd be packing in the morning and
leaving for Indented Head.

Clancy

Clancy was my best friend, even though I only ever saw him over the summer holidays. We met when we were six. Right from the start I liked him; he was stronger, louder, funnier and more adventurous than I'd ever be. I wouldn't have had such good adventures if it wasn't for him. He made me dive deeper under the wreck than I dared. He made me swim further than 'the five,' the marker that showed boats where they had to slow down to five knots. He forced me to spear innocent fish just for fun. They'd swim towards me with their big eyes wide open and I'd let loose the spear on the sea bed beneath them, while Clancy would hit a bullseye and run cavorting and dancing onto shore, holding his spear high, his dinner flapping in the breeze as it tried to free itself.

We'd sit for hours on the end of the jetty; him hauling in fish after fish while I struggled to untangle my line. He'd prattle on for hours while we waited for a bite. He'd name every fish he'd ever caught. It was a kind of ritual that he swore brought all the fish to him. Firstly, he'd draw himself up and look at the sky, then he'd take out a bag filled with bread crumbs mixed with dog food, and for every fish he named, he'd toss a handful into the sea and chant in a monotone: thirty-five whiting, nineteen bream, fourteen snapper, eighteen bluefin. Then he'd finish with a flourish, calling up all the sea creatures from the murky depths:

'Come all you fishies
Onto my hook
Then home in a bucket
For Mum to cook.'

It wasn't exactly Shakespeare, but the fish always took the bait. Sometimes he'd fill me in on all the park gossip he'd collected, moving from one caravan to another, doing his 'good-morning' rounds. He just assumed everyone liked him, and they did, with his big open smile and easy talk. One time, when I was struggling with a knot while I listened to him, he grabbed my line in frustration, cut it, re-thread it, and called me a 'fumbled fingered fish cake.' I attempted to save face by drawing attention to the fact that my parents didn't own a boat and that my dad wouldn't know a fish hook if he stepped on one. I said, "The only reason you catch so many fish is 'cos your dad takes you out on his boat every morning and you sing voodoo rhymes!"

"So what?" shot back Clancy, "Your mum's a witch, banging that drum at night."

It was true, Mum did get into a bit of djembe playing at night and improvised a bit of chanting. She said that we should all get back to our roots, "to Mother Africa, from whence we all came." Given the peculiar shade of pink she turned every summer, I had trouble believing any of her ancestors came from anywhere even remotely near Africa. None-the-less, I had to defend her honour, so I shoved Clancy off the jetty. He disappeared under his hat which eventually filled with water and sank. I waited and waited. 'Shit', I thought, 'he's gotten tangled in his own line.' I dived in and swam all around the jetty. The current was strong and it could have carried him out. I ran back to camp. I burst into the annex of his caravan, screaming "Help! Mrs. Andrews, I've killed Clancy!" She looked at me blankly and pointed inside the caravan.

"I don't think so. He's eating a sausage."

There sat Clancy, all smug with a sizzly snag in his hand. He must have dived under the jetty, crept up the rocks behind me and then run back along the road behind the boat sheds. I slapped the sausage out of his hand and stormed out.

At night Clancy would drag me out to go floundering with Aaron. With lights attached to our heads and rock shoes on, we'd tiptoe through the murky shallows, silent as snakes in the dead quiet of a black night, alone in each other's company. I'd watch the baby stingrays slip over my feet. I'd creep with my heart in my throat and a knot in my stomach. Not a night went by when I wasn't certain that I was going to die.

Just as Clancy tested my resolve in the real world, I tested his in the world of imagination. On nights when we stood on more banjo sharks than rocks, and the cool night air caressed our faces with its soft fingers, I'd whisper strange sounds and draw his attention to red eyes in the scrub off shore. Viper fish never bothered him, but vampires did.

"Look, on shore, in the scrub."

"What?"

"You know what; red eyes."

"I can't see anything."

"If you can't see them, you're marked, you're the one," I'd taunt.

"You see anything Aaron?" Aaron would look to shore.

"Yeah, two pairs of red eyes in the scrub."

"Don't move," I'd whisper.

We'd stand still for the longest time, letting the stingrays slip over our feet, until I felt I'd tormented Clancy for long enough. "They're gone. We'd better go back while it's still safe." Then we'd creep back along the shoreline, steering clear of the bushes.

Harry

Harry gingerly lifted the hatch on the roof of his caravan and poked his head out, the metal pot on his head was protection from bombs and bird droppings. He heaved himself up to his waist, steadied his shotgun and fired a loud blank high into the branches of the great Cyprus tree shading his van, sending a flock of pink breasted galahs towards the morning sun. He hated their pink breasts which were so much like splatters of blood on pale flesh. He hated any camper who wore a pink top, or a red t-shirt, or anything that reminded him of blood, and it took all of his self-control not to take pot-shots at them with his rubber bullets. He contented himself with a few seagulls serenely bobbing on calm waters close to shore; there one minute and gone the next. He sent them sinking to the ocean floor. Then he'd yell, "I love the smell of bacon in the morning; it smells like victory," his version of his favourite line from his favourite film; 'Apocalypse Now.'

I used to like to listen to the sound of the waves early in the morning as I drifted in and out of consciousness. Sometimes they made soft repetitive shushing sounds as they shivered onto shore. They would lull me back into half-forgotten dreams of a white whale tossing me high into the air on its jet of spray. At other times the waves pounded the shore, making a mockery of yesterday's sand castles. Those waves were the drums of war beating to the thud of my own heart as I clambered out of a trench, clutching a rifle, ready to face the enemy, but before I could be killed I'd always wake up. I'd yawn and stretch and think about getting up. Then Mum would swing open the door of our caravan leading to the annex where I slept, and shout, "Wakey, wakey, hands off snakey!" Then she'd roar with laughter and say it again even louder, like she wanted the whole park to hear. I'd scramble out of my sleeping bag and sprint to the toilet block, but I sometimes got ambushed by a pod of eight-year-olds with their skinny arms flaying about, making lewd gestures and chanting, "Wakey, wakey, hands off snakey." I'd slam the toilet door shut.

Harry had fought in Vietnam. He hadn't wanted to go, but he got conscripted. He started camping at Indented Head when he got back, in the early seventies. Sometimes when the light faded and it got too dark to see a cricket ball, we'd all wander over to Harry's van and he'd tell us war stories. They were the kind of stories little kids shouldn't hear, but Harry said that it was history and we all ought a know about it. He told us about the time he was crawling on his belly through the jungle and half of his unit were high on heroin or weed and he was shaking with fear, but his head was clear. He told us never to do drugs, that they'd, "kill ya quicker than any bullet." As he was crawling, he thought he saw something move in the undergrowth up ahead, and if he didn't see it, he must have sensed it, 'cos he stopped cold, shivering as he sweated. Then some idiot, high as a kite, pulled a trigger, and Harry let loose with the rest of them. When they were done, they checked the corpses. "Kids," he said, "They were just a bunch of kids, just like you lot."

Sometimes the younger kids would start to cry when Harry told his stories and then they'd scamper back to the safety of their own vans, where their mums would hold them close and ask them what had happened, looking for cuts or bruises. The kids would say, "Nothing, nothing happened." We all knew wars happened. Grown-ups killed each other in lands far away, while we swam and dived in the sweet waters of Port Phillip Bay. Killing was something grown-ups did; it had nothing to do with kids. We'd play war games on the cliffs, scaling the ridges 'til we reached the top. We'd shoot our enemies as they paddled to shore in their kayaks, and when we died, we got up again and did a crazy dance in the sand and chucked a rubber ball at a forgotten wicket left half-cocked on the shore.

Clancy said that if Harry had done it once, he could

do it again; shoot kids. "Maybe his bullets weren't all rubber. Dad says Harry's unhinged."

"Unhinged?" I said "You're unhinged."

Clancy shoved me "Nah, you're unhinged."

"Aaron's unhinged. Zeke's unhinged."

"You reckon your mum's unhinged?" taunted Clancy.

"Nah, she just acts unhinged."

"That new girl's unhinged."

We both stopped. We'd all noticed her. She was beautiful and strange.

Clancy stared at me defiantly. "I've seen you staring at her."

I leapt at him and got him in a headlock and forced him to the ground. "She's not unhinged. She's just thinking!"

"About what? No one can think all day. She just stands there staring out to sea. No one can stand that still for that long."

I walked off shouting "You're unhinged!"

The truth was, Clancy was right. He was often right, like he had some kind of secret pact with the universe. Whenever I caught sight of her, I couldn't take my eyes off her. It wasn't just that she was beautiful, like some silver-haired elf from Lord of the Rings, or some mythological mermaid, it was just that she had the saddest face I'd ever seen. It was like she'd been through something, or she was still going through something, like she was on her way to hell and had accidentally taken a left turn at Geelong and ended up on some obscure beach where people seemed to be perpetually happy; a place where happiness made a mockery of her sadness.

If I was honest with myself, I wasn't sure if I was truly attracted to her, or just attracted to what I didn't know about her. There was something about her that reminded me of Harry, not that they looked anything alike, it was just something under the surface.

I felt a kind of empathy for Harry. I felt he represented one of my possible futures. I knew he wasn't crazy. He just had P.T.S.D. and like so many veterans, he hadn't been diagnosed. He didn't get any help. He just coped as best he could.

The fact was that for quite a while I had been thinking about joining the army. It seemed like the perfect solution for someone who lacked a goal, a vision for the future, a game plan. It seemed like the perfect dumping ground for deadshits and dropouts, miscreants and misanthropes, and those suffering from social anxiety, which was a bit like having P.T.S.D., before you even see any action. It was the perfect place for lonely guys looking for a 'Band of Brothers.' Yeah, I'd seen the T.V. series and found it very appealing. It wasn't as if I didn't have my band of brothers down at Indented Head every summer, but joining the army would mean that I could have brothers all year round. I could stop being plagued by the 'only child syndrome,' whatever that meant. Besides, I'd spent hundreds of hours playing COD, Call of Duty, and I was way up there on the international rankings. I'd even made a bit of pocket money playing for other kids, to get their rankings up.

I liked the idea of not having to deal with big questions like, 'What am I going to do with my life?'

and 'What's the meaning of life anyway?' I liked the idea of living on the knife-edge of the moment, of dealing with nothing but survival; there's you and the enemy, life or death.

It was not that I was into notions of nationalism or fighting for the 'American way of life,' or the 'Australian way of life'; Australia being the fifty-first state of America and bound to follow big brother wherever he went, even places like Iraq which was a bit crazy, given that they didn't find any weapons of mass destruction there. Motives, motives for entry into any arena were tricky and were further fodder for argument in our family.

My parents were pacifists with foul tempers, who believed U.S. foreign policy had a few whiskers on it and maybe wasn't always relevant to the land of Oz. Mum often said, "If no one went to war, there wouldn't be any war! Just say NO!" I argued that it would only work if everyone said 'NO' at the same time, because a few tardy types could leave the rest of us in a compromised position. Then Mum would start rambling on about Gandhi and how without lifting a fist or a gun, he released India from colonial oppression. Dad would ramble on about how he had dodged the draft in Germany by declaring himself a pacifist, so he had to go and work in hospitals. I could see that at least he was consistent. Mum, on the other hand, was totally irrational, saying that if I joined the army she'd kill me a whole lot quicker than any bullet! She also threatened to post a video on YouTube of her doing her 'COD' song.

One day just to torment me, because she thought

I was addicted to video games, she videoed herself dressed up as an old woman in a grey wig, glasses and big fluffy slippers. She put on an exaggerated Kentucky accent and started tap dancing and singing:
'Them kids always saying shit
I can't make sense of half of it
Some of them's wrong
And some of them's right
Some of them kids just like to fight
In my day we'd talk about God
These days all they talk about is COD
In my day COD was a fish
These days it comes with a death wish'
Then she picked up my Xbox control and started pretending it was a gun. If she had ever posted that video, I would probably have died of humiliation quicker than being shot by any enemy.

Sometimes I fantasized about strapping a bomb to myself and marching into an enemy camp somewhere and blowing myself up. I wondered if most of those suicide bombers had mothers like mine. I wondered what made those guys do it; promises of virtuous virgins in heaven? Or were they just sad attention seekers wanting to be remembered as heroes? I remembered reading that Achilles chose a short life of glory and being remembered for a thousand years over a long life of domestic bliss. Maybe those suicide bombers were just disaffected, disenfranchised loners, ideological captives high on Captagon, looking for a band of brothers; doing anything to feel like they belonged somewhere, even for a short time.

I kept thinking about Harry's war and the dreaded

domino effect, when people thought that if Vietnam fell under Communism, then the whole world would fall. It felt like history was repeating itself and the wars in the Middle East had people fearing that the whole world would fall under some kind of crazy fundamentalism.

The fact remained, Mum's threat of posting that video was enough to make me pause and think twice about joining the army, and if I changed my mind there would always be a war somewhere, if the subtle challenges of peace got too much for me.

The only war I'd experienced at that point were the Water Bomb Wars, which erupted every New Year's Eve. Not many people remember exactly how they started but I do. I was about seven years old and it was a warm balmy evening. The sun was going down and the tide was out, exposing the rock pools and the reef. Mum was stretched out on her sun-lounge, staring out to sea, when a couple of teenagers kissing at the edge of the reef caught her eye.

"Hey Jesse, why don't you go and water bomb those teenagers out there and cool them down."

"No Mum, what if it makes them angry?"

"Rubbish, they'll love it. Here, I've got a few balloons inside, I'll fill them up with water. Go get Aaron and Clancy." So I did. By the time we got back, Mum had filled six balloons with water; two each. We picked our way over the rock pools until we were close enough to pelt the couple with our water bombs. Much to our surprise, they didn't think it was funny at all! The boy picked up a great heavy wad of seaweed, chased me and whacked me with it. Me and Clancy and Aaron went screaming back to the caravan. Mum must have anticipated the response, because in the meantime, she had run over to the shop across the road and bought about a dozen packets of balloons which she was busy filling up with water and packing into buckets. We spied the teenage boy, my assailant, running over to the shop and we guessed what he was going to buy. It was payback time! When he came back to the park, he had packets of balloons in his hands. He ran full pelt to the far end of the park. It seemed like all the bigger kids were camped down at that end, so we went and got Clancy's big brother Jack and his friend, to try and even things up. I still wasn't eager to go.

"But Mum, they're bigger than us."

"So what? You've got more ammunition. Go get 'em cowboy!" she egged us on.

So me and my mates marched down the middle of the caravan park, all five of us, carrying our buckets of water bombs, ready to face the enemy, head on. And there they were, striding towards us, a whole gang of them; the kissing kid with a couple of teenage mates, a couple of kids called Nelson and Shelton, who were probably about eight but looked at least ten, a couple of other kids called Brad and Gus, and to top it off, the Mighty Zees; about four of them 'cos the rest hadn't been born yet. There was Zeke and Zara and the twins Zed and Zeth, who were probably only about five years old at the time but looked at least seven. These days they'd make the Incredible Hulk look like a midget. About half way along the path was Harry's caravan which, as an American might say, marked the Mason/Dixon line. He must have had a feel for battle because his head popped out the top of his caravan and he shot off a blank. Flocks of pink galahs went crazy, squawking as they fled their tree. The hysterical galahs set off Clancy who screamed, "Down with the Westies," and let fly with the first bomb, hitting Zeth slap bang in the head. Zed got so angry, he let loose without taking aim and his water bomb knocked a wine glass out of the hand of a woman who was sitting outside her caravan. Wine and shards of glass went everywhere. Her husband stood up screaming, "I'll kill the bloody lot of yous!"

In the meantime, Harry had ducked down into his caravan and had come back up with a dozen eggs which he pelted at the Westies. He must have felt sorry for us underdogs. Zara glared at us and screamed as gooey yellow egg yolk ran down her face. Her brother Zeke went crazy and started pelting us with the accuracy of Shane Warne on a particularly good day. We suffered blow after blow.

My aim with a water bomb was about as good as my aim with a cricket ball; out of bounds and into the ear of one of the dads having a quiet beer, "I'll kill the bloody lot of ya! Those bloody balloons will end up in the bloody ocean and kill the bloody fish, ya bloody mongrels!" He came after us and we scattered in all directions. The only way to keep the battle going was guerrilla warfare. We dodged between the caravans, pelting the Westies from all directions and they gave us as good as they got, until they ran out of ammunition.

We kept running back to our caravan, where Mum was happily filling more and more balloons. It occurred with industrial speed:

Blow, bend, fill, knot, drop in bucket.

Blow, bend, fill, knot, drop in bucket.

I watched her work. She was a machine! But every now and then, she broke her rhythm, picked up a nice fat one and chucked it at one of the Westies running past, laughing her head off.

As the night wore on and it grew dark, the Westies became harder to see. The moon was a silver sliver. Then all of a sudden someone screamed, "Look, its Melbourne!" We all ran to the shoreline, or stood on the rocks opposite the wreck and there, way in the distance on the horizon, we could see the fireworks of Melbourne exploding into big yellow, red and blue balls of light. The mums and dads handed out sparklers and we waved them as our very own fireworks display began. Some dad must have gone to Canberra to get them because they were illegal to buy in Melbourne. Great cathedrals of cascading lights; red, gold, blue and green, exploded over our heads, etching out enormous shapes in the sky, then collapsing in on themselves like the birth of a new galaxy far, far away.

"Happy New Year!" we cried and hugged everyone in sight, even the Westies.

"We'll get ya next year," they yelled as they disappeared into the night, into the West, which was really further South, because the caravan park faced the bay to the East, but we kept the name 'Westies' because bad guys always come from the West, where the sun sets and good guys come from the East, with the pure light of sunrise. Every New Year's Eve we'd suspend our friendships and let the Water Bomb Wars rage, and the morning after, our friendships would begin again.

Years later, I learned about that night in World War One on the Somme, when the opposite happened; when the Germans and the Allies took a break from fighting and sang Christmas carols together in no man's land.

The Fancy Dress

The first Saturday after New Year's Eve was the Indented Head fancy dress. A camper with a sense of fun started it over fifty years ago, to give the poor kids who used to camp there something special to look forward to. He convinced all the grown-ups to chuck a few coins into a bucket, so that he could buy plenty of lollies for prizes. After him another family took it on for twenty years. By that stage the campers had got richer and the donations had got bigger, so half the money went to charity. By the time we got there, we couldn't believe the prizes we won.

The first year we entered, my friends and I went as the 'Jelly Gang' instead of the Kelly Gang. Mum turned us into jelly fish with a few green rubbish bags and seaweed. We shot everyone with our water pistols and won heaps of lollies. The next year, Mum turned Dad into a giant bug, using the sun-lounge cover and a couple of pencils stuck onto his head. He carried a sign: 'Grumpy Old Bugger.' He won first prize and got a bottle of whiskey and the biggest bag of lollies we'd ever seen; it kept us going all that summer. I went as 'Squirtle the Turtle,' with a washing bucket on my back. The following year Mum insisted Dad go as an Eskimo. She put an Eski on his head and drew a big black moustache under his nose. His sign read, 'Eski plus Mo equals Eskimo.' He won first prize again. Me and Aaron and Clancy went as the 'Three Amigos,' in giant sombreros. We also wore Mum's caravan curtains which she pinned into gaucho pants.

Noticing Mum's enthusiasm for the event, the lady who used to run it, came over and asked Mum if she'd like to take over. After twenty years, the lady's family had grown up and were leaving the caravan park. And so began the happy years of helping Mum pack the lolly bags.

At the beginning of each summer, Mum and I would drive to the big lolly warehouse in Geelong and buy hundreds of dollars' worth of lollies. She'd always let me choose what would go into the mix: twenty dollars' of bananas, twenty dollars' of milk bottles, twenty dollars' of sherbets, twenty dollars' of mint leaves, fifty dollars' of snakes, twenty dollars' of strawberry jellies, twenty dollars' of sours, fifty dollars' of frogs, twenty dollars' of Redskins, twenty dollars' of jelly beans, twenty dollars' of Smarties, fifty dollars' of Mars bars, twenty dollars' of butterscotch, twenty dollars' of milk teeth, twenty dollars' of liquorice, twenty dollars' of fruit tingles, twenty dollars' of Starbursts, fifty dollars' of Caramello Koalas, twenty dollars' of gummy bears and finally the crowning glory of confectionery; fifty dollars' worth of giant gobstoppers.

What was that? That was a list. What's the point of a list? Well, a list, for me, has always been a poem in transit. One item on the list bounces off another; proximity creates wider meaning. Those lolly bags weren't just a collection of random sweets, they were a cornucopia of childhood choices: Which ones to eat first? Which ones to save until last? Should you eat a sour before or after a mint leaf? Experience threw up combinations that should be left well alone. And then there was the question of timing; to scoff them off all at once, or to savour them one by one over a few days? Very few of us were good at delayed gratification at that time.

Once I'd settled on my choices at the warehouse, Mum and I would bring them back to the caravan and lay out plastic lolly-bags in rows on the bed. Ten rows across and ten rows down. It was my job to fill the bags before getting into my costume, three of each lolly in each bag. Usually, Aaron and Clancy came over to help. As we worked, we'd sing, "Three for them and one for us, three for them and one for us." Then Clancy would start up with, "Three for them, two for me, three for them and three for me." One time, I whacked him in the mouth and a slobbery red jelly frog flew out of his mouth and onto Mum's pillow.

"Now look what you've done, pick it up."

"No, you pick it up!"

"It's all gooey, it's got your spit on it!" I protested.

"Just turn the pillow over. No one will know," said Clancy and turned it over.

"Now it's stuck to the sheet ya idiot!"

Then we heard the shuffling of kids in the annex. It's a fact that kids can smell lollies from fifty kilometres away or at least fifty meters.

"Give me a lolly," calls Bryce. No one could say 'No' to Bryce. He was Aaron's little brother and everyone watched out for him.

"What do ya want?"

"A sherbet."

"I want a Caramello bear," shouted Hope, who was best friends with Bryce.

"Ya can't have one, they're special. Ya can have a gummy bear," dictated Clancy.

Then all the Zees tromped in. "Give us some lollies, go on!"

"Go away, there's too many of ya! There won't be any left for prizes." But I knew I had to feed the hounds before there was a mass invasion of the caravan, so I picked up a big handful of lollies and threw them into the annex. Kids caught some or pushed and shoved and fought for the ones on the floor. Then in walked Jack with a couple of Westies, Nelson and Shelton.

"Give us an all-day sucker, a gobstopper, the biggest big one!" demanded Jack.

"Okay," says Clancy, "Put ya hands behind ya back and open ya gob."

Then he tossed a giant gobstopper into the air, and Jack caught it in his wide-open mouth. But something strange happened; it slipped right down his gullet and lodged somewhere in his windpipe. His eyes popped out of his head and he made gasping noises and clutched at the door of the caravan. We all stared. We'd never seen anyone swallow a gobstopper that big before. Then he started to turn blue. I screamed, "Mum! Clancy's killed Jack, hurry!" Kids started screaming and scampering out of the annex. Mum pushed past them, "What's going on?" When she saw Jack, she grabbed him from behind, wrapped her arms around his diaphragm and heaved; the Heimlich manoeuvre. The bright blue gobstopper flew out of Jack's mouth with such force that it smacked Hope in the eye, leaving a deep blue stain, like she'd been hit with a cricket ball. Then it rolled out of the annex and onto the sand. Clancy chased it and washed it under the outside tap, then put it in his mouth. Jack was so mad, he punched Clancy in the stomach. The gobstopper flew out of his mouth and it rolled under the neighbour's caravan. Some of the little kids chased it and one was just about to put it into his mouth, when Mum screamed, "Leave it, leave it! Just let the bloody thing die in peace!" and she kicked sand over it.

One year, I went to the fancy dress as 'Warne Out,' a very tired Shane Warne and Dad went as 'Bossy Boots,' with dozens of shoes tied all over him. Another year me and Aaron and Clancy covered ourselves in big gnarly strands of rubbery bronze seaweed and went as the 'Three Wise Sea-Monkeys;' see no evil, speak no evil, hear no evil. One of the dads tied an electric fan to his head and played a guitar and went as 'Fan-tail of the Opera.' The next year Mum dressed up as a horse and Dad dressed up as a knight with a box on his head, the rubbish bin lid as a shield and the bread knife as a sword. The sign read, 'Welcome to my Knight-mare,' and I went as a 'Twister,' wrapped up in the Twister game, twirling like a hurricane, and doing the Twist. Then another year Mum wrapped me up in tinfoil and put a pot on my head and Clancy tied a hessian sack on his head and we went as 'Tinman and Scarecrow,' from the Wizard of Oz. Another year Mum tied me into the portable steps which made a sort of V shape so I looked like a kid in a car. Then she tied shoes around it; 'Michael Shoe-Maker,' the racing car driver. Next, she threw a green shade cloth over Dad's head and put sunglasses on top; 'Shady Character!' Clancy's dad wore a wok on his head and carried a guitar; 'Wok and Roll.' Another year Mum insisted that me and one of the Zees put collapsible camp chairs on our heads, then she hung a few old portable radios and iPods on them with music blaring full blast; 'Musical Chairs.' The next year she insisted that me and all my friends put a pair of Bonds underpants on our heads and go as 'The James Bonds, skid-marks and all.'

Every year at least one kid would come as Batman because we were camped at Batman Park, Indented Head. We all thought the park had been named after the super hero. It wasn't until I was in year ten that I realized the park was named after the explorer and founder of Melbourne, John Batman. History has it, that after slaughtering aboriginal people in the Black Wars of Tasmania in the 1820's, he took to exploring Port Phillip Bay, and at some point landed near Indented Head, where he cut a sly land deal with the natives by swapping a few tools and blankets for vast tracts of land, which he named Batmania. Melbourne could have ended up as the sister city to Gotham.

If I had been around to name the caravan park, I would have called it Buckley Park because Indented Head was also the place where the wild man, William Buckley, burst out of the bush after spending thirty years living with the aboriginal people of the area. I used to imagine what he was like; I was sure he must have been a giant. He was supposed to have been almost seven foot tall. He knew how to speak the language of the Wathaurang people and he had aboriginal wives. He knew about their culture. He knew how to find food and water in the bush. He could survive. He knew how to hunt for kangaroo and wallaby. He could throw a spear and his boomerang always came back. He knew how to cool-burn the undergrowth, so bushfires didn't spread. He knew the healing power of plants. He knew the secret rituals, and painted his face with ochre and danced the spirit dances of the animals. He stared into the flames of the campfire at night and listened to the whispered words of the ancestors. He watched their ghost bodies glide between the branches of the ghost gums. He listened to the stories of the dreamtime and knew things that no other white man would ever know. He knew the power of the bone. He knew his way home. He was a super hero. Yeah, I would have called the park

Buckley Park.

One year, after the fancy dress parade, a group of kids came over to our caravan screaming that some other kids had stolen their lollies. Well, that set Mum off. There were certain triggers that set off Mum's New York stories and anything to do with stealing or robbers was one of them.

"You've been robbed?" started Mum, "I could tell you a thing or two about robbers. There was a time when I was living on the corner of Avenue C and 7th Street in Alphabet City in the bad lands of New York City...."

The kids exchanged glances. I knew what they were thinking; that Mum was obviously making this one up. Whoever heard of a city named after the alphabet? Mum carried on regardless:

"I was sitting in my apartment, on my couch, which I had just covered in lovely pink floral material because the previous owners of the couch must have liked boring brown."

The kids looked at each other again, 'Who cares about pink flowers?' they were thinking. "Hang in there," I said, "She's just getting started." They shrugged.

"I was sitting on the pink couch under a gum tree," Mum continued. "Yep, I'd gone out and bought myself a little gum tree in a pot and put it beside the couch because I was feeling homesick. There I was peacefully reading Pride and Prejudice..."

This was turning nasty and beginning to sound like it was going to turn into one of Mum's English lessons. The kids were beginning to back out of the annex.

"When bang, the front door to the apartment crashed

to the ground and three robbers with guns burst in. One of them held his gun to my head and said, 'Where is it?'"

The kids froze and stared at Mum.

"Well being petrified, I couldn't think what to do, so I did nothing. I just kept reading my book, hoping they'd go away." Then Mum put on her best New York gangster accent:

'Did you hear me lady? Where is it?' said the robber.

'Where's what?' I replied, 'I have no idea what you're talking about.'

'You know.'

'Know what? If I knew what you were looking for, I could help you find it.'

'The gun,' said the robber.

'But you've already got a gun,' I replied.

'Not this gun,' he snarled.

'Which gun?' I queried. I was becoming annoyed. These stupid robbers obviously didn't know what they wanted.

'The gun you're hiding.'

'But I'm not hiding a gun. I'm reading Pride and Prejudice, it's really very good. Have you read it?' I enquired. Well, obviously the stupid robber wasn't into literature, so he ordered the other two robbers to look for the missing gun. They ransacked the entire apartment, pulled out all the drawers, emptied the cupboards, turned over the beds and threw everything onto the floor.

'There's nothing here,' said one of the robbers.

This made the gangster holding the gun to my head very annoyed. 'Where is it?' he demanded and pressed the gun even harder to my temple.

'I think we've had this conversation before,' I said patronisingly."

Then at that moment in the story, something terrible happened, not terrible for Mum but terrible for the robbers. The more often I had heard that story, the more sympathy I'd had for the robbers and the less sympathy I had for my mother.

"At that moment one of the robbers glanced up at a wall covered in theatre posters, above the dining room table, and recognized me," continued Mum.

"'Is that you?' he asked.

'Well of course it's me. They're all me.'

'Aw. Are you an actress?'

'A theatre actress. They're theatre posters,' I said as calmly as I could and walked over to the wall. The robber with the gun followed close behind. The three robbers stood on one side of the table pointing their guns at me, while I stood on the other side pointing to the various posters and giving them an insight into each of the theatre productions; plot-lines and characters. There's nothing quite like an attentive audience! I don't know if it was nerves, or that I'd simply warmed to my topic but once I'd started, I simply couldn't stop:

'I love this first play. It tells the story of a man who's in jail and about to be hung. His sister comes to visit him and they relive the story of their childhood; two lonely kids without a mother, brought up by a drunken father, clinging to each other for comfort. The play was so intense with just a hint, an undercurrent, of sexual tension. It was later turned into a telemovie! Now this next poster was for a play that tells the story of a blues singer, her trials, her triumphs; fabulous songs! Would you like to hear one?' I asked them. The robbers nodded. Their arms seemed to be getting tired and their guns were drooping, so I gave them an excellent rendition of one of the blues songs from the show.

'Both those plays got excellent reviews in the New York Times. Do you read reviews?' I quizzed the robbers and one of the robbers shook his head and mumbled, 'Ah no, not very often,' so I continued on:

'Now this third play is one of my favourites. The funny thing is, it did extremely well in Australia but it bombed in New York. I'm not saying that I, personally, didn't get a nice review in The New York Times, but the critic disliked the writing. I love the story. It's set in the early nineteenth century and tells the tale of an intense relationship between two sisters and their manservant stranded on an Island, off the coast of Australia. I wore a lovely faded apple green embroidered gown, and I had to gut a huge fish in the very first scene. We used a real fish every night! Well, we were performing eight times a week! On Saturday afternoons we'd get the 'bridge and tunnel' crowd, the oldies, the retirees from the outer suburbs. Well, one Saturday we were nearing the end of the play and I was doing my big death scene, which usually took about ten minutes and had the audience in tears, but on this particular occasion the silence was punctuated by a broad Jersey accent: 'George, George what happened to the fish?' The old lady must have thought she was watching T.V. and nobody could hear her! The audience started to titter. I caught the other actress's eye and we both did our best to stifle our laughter. As I lay in bed dying, she thoughtfully pulled a blanket over my head so the audience wouldn't see me laughing and to signal that I had finally died.'

'Where's the fish?' mimicked one of the robbers, laughing. By this stage all three of them had lowered their guns. 'That's funny lady but we have to go.'

'But I haven't finished yet! There's only a few more posters to go!' and I started in on the next play: 'We did this one at a wonderful little downtown theatre called Theatre for the New City and we got absolutely fabulous reviews in the New York Times! You'll love this one. It's real bad boy stuff. It's about a boxer who killed his girlfriend and her ghost comes back to haunt him. Great songs, really great songs. Would you like to hear one?'

'Aw, sorry lady we've got to go,' said the head robber and they started to back out towards the door. When they reached it, they turned and ran down the stairs.

I chased them and called out from the top of the stairs, 'Come back I haven't finished yet!' but they just kept running."

Sometimes when I listened to my mother telling her stories, those tales from her past life, the life she'd led before she had me, I felt like I didn't know her. It was as if she was somebody else, from somewhere else, and the life she lived with me wasn't her real life; it was just a pretend life, and I thought that one day she'd pack up and leave and start living her real life, the life she lived before me.

By that time there were only a few kids left in the annex. The others had quietly slipped away while Mum was immersed in her story. She looked at the few that were left and said, "So, if you are ever attacked by robbers, the best thing to do is just bore them to death. At the time I felt a bit like that girl from 'A Thousand and One Nights', who saved her life by telling the king a different story every night."

"But where was the gun?" asked one of the kids.

"What gun?" queried Mum.

"The gun you were hiding."

"I wasn't hiding a gun," said Mum.

"Why didn't you scream and run away?" asked another kid.

"I was paralysed; paralysed with fear. All I could do was act normal. I thought that if I'm going to die, at least I'll die reading a good book or talking about one of my productions."

"But what about our lollies? What are we supposed to do about them?" asked Bryce, "Are we supposed to go and bore the robbers?"

"I've got a better idea," said Mum, "I've got a few extra bags of lollies, let's go and see if they want some more."

Mum had carried out this experiment when I was about five. She had bought a big bag of lollies for me and my school friend, Fred, and told us to go outside and share them out equally. I took the bag and started to share them out, "One for me and one for you, one for me and one for you." All of a sudden Fred grabbed one of my lollies and shoved it in his mouth. I continued, "One for you and one for me." Every time I put down a lolly for me, he snatched it and stuffed it in his mouth. I ran inside; "Mum, Fred's not sharing."

"Give him a lolly, one at a time," said Mum.

"But then I won't have any," I complained.

"Watch what happens." So I ran outside and said, "Do you want another lolly, Fred?" He grabbed it and shoved it into his gob. "Do you want another one?"

"Yep," he said and shoved another one into his mouth.

I kept going until Fred's cheeks were bloated with lollies and multi-coloured dribble was coming out of his mouth, but he was grinning happily. I kept giving him lollies and when he couldn't get any more into his mouth, he put them in his bag. Finally I ran out of lollies; "I haven't got any more left Fred." He just looked at me and then the tears started to roll down his face. He spat out a big glob of chewed up lollies, then dropped his bag on the ground.

"I don't want any more lollies."

I picked up the bag, "It's okay, we can share them out again equal, one for you and one for me."

At bed time that night, I asked Mum what had happened. I didn't get it. She said that I was doing all the giving and Fred was doing all the taking, and that maybe in the end it made him feel weak.

I watched the kids carrying the remaining lolly bags over to the playground where the robbers were. I watched them hand out the lollies, one by one. I heard one kid say, "Would you like another one?"

On the topic of lollies, it's impossible to think about them or talk about them without remembering my mother's unconventional attitude to Halloween. The truth was, it was never part of Aussie culture until about twenty years ago, when there was some kind of revolution after a critical mass of kids had seen enough American movies to figure out that they were missing out on a whole heap of fun. Thousands of kids hounded their parents to let them go out 'Trick or Treating,' dressed in ghoulish gear.

After lecturing me on the evils of adopting American customs, and hammering home the idiocy of celebrating a Northern hemisphere autumn harvest festival during an Aussie' spring, Mum embraced the tradition with gusto, justifying her enthusiasm by equating Halloween to both All Souls Eve and The Day of the Dead. She saw it as a perfect opportunity to, "teach the little buggers that life isn't all 'beer and skittles' nor is it all laughter and lollies and giving a kid a good fright now and then prepares them for reality!" So every Halloween, Mum would dress up as a particularly ugly witch with fake blood drooling from the corners of her mouth. She would then fill a big basket full of fake lollies, usually baby onions, exquisitely wrapped in colourful lolly paper. She also carried another basket full of frozen peas. She'd sit behind the front door waiting for the bands of unsuspecting kids to knock. When she heard them chant 'Trick or Treat' she'd slam open the door and screech, "TRICK! I WANT A TRICK!" The kids would just stare at her with their mouths open. They were ill-prepared for the unexpected. None of them ever thought to bring a trick. Grown-ups were meant to smile sweetly and give them lollies. Sometimes younger kids would burst out crying, and Mum would screech,

"Wash ya hands and do not sneeze or all you'll get from me are PEAS!" Then she'd pelt them with frozen peas which made the younger kids howl even harder because frozen peas hurt. Mum soon figured out that it was important to defrost peas before terrorising children. Then, to placate them, she'd offer them a nice big 'lolly' and say, "These are magic lollies, I made them myself this morning. If you open them now they'll turn into onions, but if you keep them under your bed for six months they'll turn into fairy dust, and then if you plant that dust in the garden and make a wish, it'll come true within two years." Dozens of kids, who were incapable of delayed gratification, would open their lollies and start complaining that they were only onions! So Mum would screech, "I told you they would turn into onions! Now look what you've done!" Then Mum would slam the door shut in their faces and wait for the next group of unsuspecting kids to come along.

Mum carried out this tradition year after year, after year, after year. She just wouldn't stop! Even now she says she can't stop because the kids look forward to it. And they do, they just keep coming back and some years there's a queue stretching all the way down the street.

One year, the day after Halloween, Mum found a card in the letterbox with a picture of a witch on the front. When she opened it, a kid had written: 'Dear Pea witch, thank you so much for being so mean to us.' Strangely enough, after about ten years, a teenager knocked on the door one Halloween, dressed as a vampire. She said that when she was nine, she kept her magic lolly and didn't open it for six months and true to Mum's word, when she did open it, the paper was filled with green dust, so she buried it in the garden and made a wish, and to her surprise, about one year later, her wish came true! Mum begged her to tell what the wish was, but the girl just shook her head and refused, saying that it was bad luck to tell anybody a wish. Then the girl asked me if my mum was really a witch. I said that I couldn't be sure, but every year around Halloween, her nose did look a little longer, her eyes a little darker and she sometimes had a little bit of blood on her teeth.

The Dumb Family

"There goes the fat family." That's what my father used to say. He'd sit there all day, hanging shit on anyone who walked past our camp site, but he was always careful to keep his voice down so the passers-by never heard him.

"What are we Dad? The dumb family? Dumb, dumber and dumbest?"

"Don't calling me dumb!" he'd retaliate in his peculiar grammar.

"I'm not calling you dumb, I'm calling you dumbest." That'd get him really worked up. The truth was I sometimes hated his guts. He didn't go to work. He didn't seem to care about anyone except himself. He was German. He seemed to have some inbuilt sense of superiority. He thought that he was better than everybody else. I used to think he was some sort of reincarnation of Goebbels, which probably wasn't fair given that his own dad had been a communist and could have ended up in a concentration camp, if he hadn't been working on the docks building U-boats for the Führer.

Dad would sit in front of the caravan thinking for a couple of weeks. Then, if I was lucky, he'd pack up and go back to the city, saying he was bored and that he'd had an idea for a work of art, which meant Mum and I would have the rest of the holidays to ourselves and I wouldn't have to listen to my parents fighting all summer.

They used to fight over what plates to use, whether to rinse them under the cold tap or pile them up and wash them under the hot water in the laundry at the end of the day. They'd fight over where to sit or who ate the last banana, or what music to play, or whose turn it was to put up the gazebo, or whose turn it was to cook, or the military situation in the Middle East, or the political situation in the United States, or the environmental situation on the Great Barrier Reef, or the financial situation in Europe, or the food crisis in Africa, or the degradation of the Antarctic, or the lampooning of Putin in Russia, or the Jihad in Jalalabad, or Orientalism in Oz. My parents argued about everything from the setting on the toaster to the conflict in Syria and gave equal vehemence to each. I grew up thinking there was a fundamental connection between land mines and toasters, and in a pinch a person could make a land mine out of a toaster. Every topic or any topic was food for a fight, augmented with argument. My parents were the casualties of conflict and me, the collateral damage. They argued over everything!

I remember one year a hot northerly wind was blowing and Mum and Dad were bickering about rubbish disposal. Dad insisted that food scraps should be put into a separate bin, while Mum argued that the caravan park didn't separate its rubbish and food rubbish was tossed in with all the other rubbish. With that, Mum chucked an entire lettuce, that had gone brown, into our bin. Then Dad, in a fit of defiance, lunged into the bin and retrieved the sorry looking lettuce, yelling that he was going to feed it to the seagulls. Mum was adamant that seagulls did not eat lettuce and begged Dad not to be a moron for once in his life. "Don't you calling me a moron!" Dad protested in the kind of grammar that added fuel to Mum's fire. Then he stormed out of the annex and into the sea.

It was one of those forty-degrees days and the wind was blustery. The beach was packed and even the oldies were wading up to their waists. Dad started peeling off lettuce leaves and tossing them in all directions calling, "Here birdie, birdie" and making bizarre attempts at seagull squawks, that sounded more like a cat being strangled. Mum hid in the caravan, while I peeked out from the annex. The hot northerly wind picked up the lettuce leaves and blew them in all directions. One large leaf flew out of Dad's hand and planted itself on the face of an old lady gingerly wading into the water. She screamed in horror as she tried to wrench it off.

Her aging husband, in a fit of chivalry, tried to wrestle the offending lettuce out of Dad's hand and in the tussle tripped and almost drowned. Luckily someone helped him to shore, while Dad, oblivious, continued to scatter more leaves while lecturing the crowd on the importance of composting food waste. I watched the lettuce leaves floating benignly on the swell, untouched by any gulls, and carefully avoided by swimmers searching for more hospitable waters. The fact was, Dad was an embarrassment.

Once, when Dad returned from the city to help pack-up camp, we took a long walk together to St Leonards to get an ice cream. Dad loved ice cream. He said his family hardly ever had it when he was a kid because they were so poor. I asked him what he did when he went back to Melbourne, what he did without me and Mum. I imagined he was an ex-SS soldier running from justice, hiding in Australia to escape war crime investigations. I immersed myself in the history and mythology of the Third Reich. I felt guilty about things I didn't do. I felt guilty by association, by a quirk of DNA. I felt that my father wasn't who he said was. I forgot that he was only three years old when the war ended. To me he was a man with secrets. I eye-balled him.

"Vy do you look at me like that? Are you constipated?" he questioned me. Why did my parents always reduce everything to the lowest common denominator?

"No, I just want to know who you are," I replied.

"I am your father."

"I want to know who you really are. I don't believe you just go back to Melbourne to paint. You don't seem to produce many paintings."

"It's qvality not qvuantity," he argued.

I thought about a kid at school who said his dad was having an affair. I looked at my father and for a moment I didn't trust him. He looked like a man who had affairs. "Do you love Mum?"

"She is a very annoying person."

"That doesn't answer my question."

"She gets on my nerves."

"I asked Mum if you had affairs and she said, 'Why would any man look at another woman if he had me?'"

My father laughed, "You see, she is impossible but she is correct. Other vimen don't interest me." I breathed a sigh of relief. At least he wasn't a cheat, but I still didn't know who he was. He hardly ever talked about Germany or why he left. Maybe he hadn't gassed people but he could still have been running from something.

We finally made it to St Leonards and got our ice cream, Dad's favourite, Pistachio, double scoop. We sat on the end of the pier and I watched him savour every lick like he had never tasted it before. He closed his eyes and licked some more. He didn't like to be disturbed when was eating Pistachio. The truth was, I didn't think Pistachio was that great, but I always got it when I was with Dad to try and pretend that we had something in common, or maybe just as a sign of solidarity, to let him know I didn't actually blame him for my German heritage.

I liked sitting with him. We hardly ever hung out together. When I was a kid, he used to get bored playing kick the kick with the footy and when I asked him to bowl a cricket ball, so that I could practice my batting, he went to a sports shop and bought me a cricket ball attached to a rope and hung it from a tree in our backyard. He said that I didn't need anyone to bowl to me and I could practice by myself. The trouble was, when I whacked the hanging ball good and hard, it swung back and nearly knocked my head off.

The fact was, Dad didn't like to do anything but paint. I remember one time he set up an easel for me in the garage with a blank canvass on it, right next to his. He squirted a whole lot of colours onto a palette, then he handed me a brush and nodded at the canvas. He got on with his own painting while I stared at the blank canvas, nothing happened. After a while Dad just forgot about me, so I wandered back inside.

I remember once I asked him if he was a ghost. He used to float around the house with a blank look on his face. Sometimes he'd walk straight past me without seeing me. At other times he'd look straight through me as if I wasn't there. Sometimes he made me feel like I was a ghost. One day I asked my mother if I was a ghost. She was piling a load of washing into the washing machine and said that ghosts didn't leave dirty underwear on the bathroom floor! Dad floated past on his way to the toilet.

On the pier, Dad laughed when I reminded him, of the time I'd asked him if he was a ghost. He said that sometimes he felt like a ghost and that it was hard to make a life in a foreign country. He said that it wasn't easy to speak English and he knew that everyone thought he was dumb. He couldn't make what was in his head come out of his mouth and when his friends cracked jokes, he didn't always know what they were laughing about. He hardly ever talked about his family; his mum and dad, his brother and sister. He forgot that they were my grandparents, my aunty and uncle, my family too. It was as if he wanted to forget something; something that I wanted him to remember.

When he'd finished eating his ice cream, he stood up, "Ve go back."

"Can't we stay a bit longer?" I pleaded. He took off his shoes and dangled his legs over the side of the pier. For once he didn't seem to be in a hurry to be somewhere else. "Do you ever think that you should have stayed in Germany?" I asked him.

"If I'd stayed in Germany you vouldn't be here."

"Yeah, but do you sometimes wish you'd stayed?"

"Yes, yes but coming here vos a great adventure. I followed the old hippie trail. I travelled overland to Greece, then by boat to Istanbul. From Istanbul to Tehran, from Tehran to Kabul, from to Kabul to Delhi and from Delhi I sailed by boat across the Bay of Bengal, then travelled on to Indonesia and finally took a small boat to Darvin."

Dad stared dreamily out to sea, lost in some place I'd never been to. "In Istanbul I got lost in a narrow maze of streets. I slept in doorways and begged for food in the marketplaces. I feasted my eyes on the colours of a million spices, pigments for paintings. The aromas pierced my nostrils and made my head dizzy. I dozed in the sun beside the great Hagia Sophia and crept inside the Blue Mosque. I valked barefoot across the mosaics of a million blue tiles. I spun in circles and marvelled at the hundreds of blue stained-glass vindows and vhen I stopped spinning, I lifted my eyes to the great blue domes above me and tried to imagine the meaning of the calligraphy that floated above me in bands of blue. I'll take you there one day, and ve vill vhisper and spin together in the home of another man's god."

I stared at him, I didn't want him to stop, he'd never said we could do anything together before, let alone travel to exotic places. "Where did you go after that?" I prompted him.

"From Istanbul I travelled to Tehran, a huge city that sits beneath snowcapped mountains. I vashed my hands in the blue pool outside the Royal Palace and gazed up at the mountains that towered above. It was a city full of universities and bazars. Back then the old Sha had banned veils and vimen vore vestern clothes. They were sophisticated and vell educated. I hiked the mountain trails vith groups of students. Ve had picnics, ve laughed. It vos on one of those picnics that I met Ted, the American. He'd been on the trail for a few years dodging the draft. He had turned down the U.S. government's invitation to see the sites of Vietnam. The years on the road had left him looking scruffy. His long blond hair swung across his back as he valked, his baggy pants vere torn and his bright orange kaftan had a few stains but the young vimen loved him. He made them laugh. Vimen love men who make them laugh. Ted's idea vos to seduce as many young vimen as he could from as many different countries as he could. I liked him too, because he made me laugh. For him life vos just one big joke. He used to laugh at my English but it got better. I remember there vos a girl. She didn't look at Ted, she looked at me. She vos studying medicine but vhen I said I was leaving, she didn't vont to leave Tehran and come vith me, she vonted to finish her degree. At the Grand Bazar, I haggled over the price of a gold bracelet, a parting gift. It was there ve heard vhispers that the old Sha's time vos up. There vould be a new ruler. The rumblings of revolution were starting. The students vere scared about losing their freedom if there vos a change. Ted and I left one morning vithout saying goodbye."

I wondered what happened to the girl. Dad always seemed to leave bits out. I guessed he wasn't going to take me to Tehran, but it didn't matter as long as he kept talking to me. I just hoped that he was talking to me and not just talking to himself.

"From Tehran I travelled to Kabul vhere blue shapeless figures bought food in the marketplaces vhile their men stood by, varily vatching the vandering eyes of strangers. I ate dates and drank tea in the cafés vith those men and vhen one man invited me to his home for a meal, ve vere served by a silent blue ghost; his vive. The food vos good and the sight of a slim wrist stirred me. Vhen I lifted my head and met her eyes, they were blue, a greenish blue, they startled me. I smiled and she floated back into the kitchen. Her husband pointed to a photo of Hitler on the vall and grinned. Maybe he thought that all Germans vere Nazis. He tried to persuade me to join the ranks of a right-ving revolutionary group. I tried to explain that

I was left-ving but he vould not listen. He asked me to stay the night but I said I had to go. Veeks past and people stared as Ted and I drifted through the narrow alleyways to visit the hashish dens, vhere Ted had been many times before. Ve talked, ve smoked, ve laughed and my English got better. In that haze of smoke, ve imagined that ve understood the mysterious language of the Afghanis who smoked and laughed beside us. From Kabul, ve made our way to Delhi. It was Ted's favourite part of the journey. Ve picked up a couple of beautiful Swedish girls along the vay. Ve all practised English together."

I stared at my father. I read between the lines. I could imagine what 'practising English' meant. I guessed that my father wasn't exactly a practising virgin on the hippie trail. He said that when they reached Delhi, it was hot and crowded. The four of them shared one small room in a hostel to save money. They started to argue. Dad said that Ted got jealous, because the girl he was with wanted to be with Dad. In the end they all got on Dad's nerves, so he left and went to Kathmandu while the other three travelled south to Goa, which was supposed to be the great hippie haven of free love and almost free drugs. Dad said that a few months later he found out that Ted had overdosed. Dad always thought that they would meet up again one day on the trail. I wondered what happened to the Swedish girls.

Ted's death made Dad think about his own mortality, so he washed himself in the sacred waters of the great Ganges River, then made his way to an ashram in Kathmandu, to try and get more in touch with his soul.

The guru there told him that he too was a wise man. One day when they were meditating together, a brick toppled off the top of the old ashram building and hit Dad on the head. He said that was the moment his third eye opened and he could see the world more clearly.

I used to stare at Dad's forehead and try to see his third eye. He said that I couldn't see it because it was under the skin. I sometimes wondered if Dad's third eye had a cataract because he didn't seem very wise to me. In the end, I figured out that Dad probably never had a third eye, he'd probably just had concussion. Anyway at that time, Dad's third eye let him know that it was time to leave the ashram, so he travelled down south to a little seaside town called Pondicherry, where he joined the crew of a Frenchman, who was sailing his old yacht across the Bay of Bengal to Malaysia, and that's when Dad's troubles really kicked off.

A couple of days out to sea, it became obvious that Dad wasn't the only crew member who had never sailed before and that the captain had chosen his crew according to beauty, not experience. So there was Dad, with three girls, one from Argentina and two from Italy. The only language they all had in common was English and no one could speak it very well. There were a lot of ropes and a lot of orders and a lot of misunderstandings. The girls kept complaining about the conditions, the food, the work, and the captain kept trying to sleep with all three of them. After a while Dad lost track of time and it seemed that his third eye wasn't doing its job, because just as he was thinking about abandoning ship and swimming to shore, no matter how far away it was, a great storm blew up and raged all night. In all the confusion, the crew didn't pull down the sails fast enough and the gale ripped right through them and snapped the mast. The boat tossed and turned, totally at the mercy of the sea. Dad said that he held the beautiful Argentinian girl in his arms and prepared to die, but when morning finally came, the boat had washed-up on the shores of Burma.

By the time he'd got through telling me about sailing across the Bay of Bengal, Dad had done enough sharing for one day. He stood up and stretched. He was a man still proud of his physique. With his back erect and his jaw jutting forward he pronounced "Ve go," and I knew my time was up. We walked all the way back to camp in silence, which I didn't mind because I was lost in my own thoughts, my own fantasies of all the far-away places I would explore when the time came.

I had no idea where all those places were, those places that my father had been to, but I loved the sound of the names of the cities; Istanbul, Tehran, Kabul, Delhi. When I got home that summer, I looked them up and travelled with my fingers across the atlas. I vowed that I would go to all those places myself one day.

Australia Day

On Australia Day, we'd wake to the loud belch of motorbikes. Bands of fat men dressed in black leather jackets and black Nazi helmets riding big black bikes, gunned their way down to St Leonards for the day; 'born to be wild' at fifty kilometres an hour, each a legend in his own mind. 'Born to be Wild,' yeah, Mum had made me watch the movie. The bikies would have a counter lunch of steak and chips, or Surf 'n Turf and guzzle beer all afternoon, before riding the lonely highway home, red-eyed and over the limit.

The park filled with all sorts of extras on Australia Day. Uncles, aunties, cousins and friends filled the place. Swirling shrieks of laughter reverberated from every caravan and tent. The gut-wrenching smell of onions, sausages, bacon, steak and chops browning on a hundred barbecues drove me wild, while Dad threw another lump of tofu on the barbie.

"Dad, please not today! Just one sausage," I pleaded.

"I am a vegetarian."

"Well I'm not, Mum's not."

"I don't care. I eat tofu in solidarity vith the Aborigines," said Dad, self-righteously.

"The Aborigines didn't eat tofu, they ate kangaroo," growled Mum.

"Yeah, let's go get some kanga burgers," I pleaded.

"No," insisted Dad, "people shouldn't celebrate genocide."

"They are not celebrating genocide. They are celebrating a successful multicultural society," argued Mum.

"That incarcerates it's native population and is guilty of an alarming number of black deaths in custody," retorted Dad.

"Dad, I just want a sausage," I begged.

"Sausages are a symbol of British colonialism and vhite oppression over the black man." Dad declared.

"Oh shut-up," snarled Mum, "Sausages are German. You lot brought them over here. They're a symbol of German gluttony!"

"Mum, Dad! We're all on the same side! I just want a burger."

"Yeah, the barbecues are driving me crazy. C'mon Jesse, we're going to Portarlington," Mum rallied, in a moment of mutiny.

Then off we went, leaving Dad with his tofu. We bought burgers with the lot and sat high on the hill overlooking the pier at Port, right next to the people from the Classic Car Club, who often picnicked there on Australia Day. They showed off their perfectly preserved vintage Ford Mustangs and Thunderbirds or Corvett Sting Rays. There were old Rolls-Royces, Buicks, Dodges, Pontiacs, Cadillacs, and heaps of Holdens: 1950's FXs and FJs, 1960's FBs, EHs and EKs, 1968 Monaros, 1970's Kingswoods and Statesmen, 1980's Commodores and 1990 Caprices. They were painted in every colour from irritating apricot to aggravating aqua, with a few garish purples in between, each worth tens of thousands of dollars.

As I chomped on my burger, Mum worked her way through her Australia Day lecture:

"These cars aren't just machines, they're symbols; symbols of a bygone era, when Australia was the richest country in the world per capita, when we had a robust manufacturing industry, when we showed the world that multiculturalism, a fair-go and an eight-hour working day led to peace and prosperity. That was before clever Ford and Toyota and Mazda divided the industry. The Holden was our car. It looked great and it was reliable. We always had a Holden when I was growing up."

"Mum, Ford closed in Geelong and Toyota closed in Adelaide. Heaps of people lost their jobs! We don't have a car industry, so what are you babbling about!" I protested.

"I'm just saying I like old Holdens. They're beautiful. Look at the apricot one!"

Mum wiped the tomato sauce off the side of her mouth with the back of her hand and suggested I do the same, but I left my Australia Day war paint on as preparation for the next round of battle, which was bound to erupt the moment we returned to camp. But when we got back, Dad just lifted his head from his sketch book and looked right through us, without saying a word. Mum walked straight past him, as if she hadn't seen him. Their silence was deafening. I liked it better when they fought.

Pelicans

The pelicans sat in stately silence, patiently riding the swell, waiting for the nightmare of knuckleheads on jet skis to end. I watched them from our site, envious of their speed, and I watched the girl. Her silver hair cascaded down her back and almost touched the sand as she sat on the shoreline with her head resting on her knees; the water lapping at her ankles. The noise of the jet skis didn't seem to bother her.

"Stupid drongos!" yelled Mum, "Polluting the bay with their noise and petrol fumes. Stupid fuckwits."

Mum didn't see eye to eye with men on jet skis. I tried to explain that in an age where men no longer galloped fast and free on mighty steeds across open plains, jet skis were magnificent, heroic water-horses, on which a man could test his courage and satisfy his need-for-speed.

"Bullshit!" said Mum, "They're just big mechanical dicks, for dim-witted drongos, who don't give a shit about anyone but themselves and probably can't get a girlfriend and probably never will, because girls hate fuckwits who ride jet skis!"

The pelicans patiently waited for the drongos to depart, so they could dive and duck beneath the surface of the water, then with fish in bill, fly away with the prize, wings a fathom wide, they'd flap and rise. The girl lifted her head and watched them fly. She watched them until they were almost out of sight. And out of sight, I watched her from our caravan.

My mother once told me that when I was six months old, I rolled out of the beach towel I was wrapped in and straight into a pelican's bill. Too big to swallow, it spat me out, a screaming mass of squalling slime. Mum wiped me down and held me close and whispered that the bird was just playing, but I've side-stepped them ever since. They're smarter than you think.

One night when I was a kid, I came back to the caravan to find that Mum was gone. I waited and waited. I imagined that she had been kidnapped, or that something bad had happened. I worried about what would happen to me if she didn't come back. I wondered if I could survive without her. I thought about all those kids in refugee camps, in war zones, who didn't have anyone, whose parents had been killed. I thought about all those kids whose lives were worse than mine and

I knew that I would be okay. Then, just when I had stopped myself from worrying about myself, Mum skipped in and said that it was a great night to take a hike in the moon light.

Even when I was older, I worried about me; what would become of me and what I would become. I was good at science but the truth was, I didn't care about maths and microbes or the difference between meiosis and mitosis. Everyone else my age seemed to know where they were going and what they were doing, but I was just confused. One day I wanted to be an astronaut, the next day I wanted to be an actor, then I wanted to be a neuroscientist and the day after that I wanted to be a writer. A few days later I wanted to be a spy or a musician. There were so many things that I wanted to be, so many things I wanted to do, and so many things I didn't want to be and so many things I didn't want to do.

Ever since I was eight, I'd suffered dizzy spells any time I'd thought about who or what I was, or why I was here, or how I got here or what the hell we were all meant to be doing here. Sometimes I would paddle way out past 'the five,' when the water was flat and quiet in the morning, and I'd just think and think until I couldn't think anymore. Then my head would begin to ache and I'd paddle back.

"You're white as a sheet," Mum would say.

"I've got a headache. I feel dizzy."

"That's not a headache, that's existential angst," Mum would console me. "You need to read Jean-Paul Sartre's 'Nausea' or Camus' 'The Outsider.'"

Every time I had a problem, my mother would add another book to my reading list.

Any compliment from Mum was often followed fast with an insult. "Oh god, you are brilliant rowing out to the five." But on spying my sodden bathers on the bed she'd scream "You bloody idiot! Don't you have a brain in your head? What's the matter with you people?" 'You people,' always referred to males. According to Mum's cosmological paradigm, we were definitely from another planet, yet Mum seemed to love every boy in the caravan park. She was always chatting to them, or looking into their buckets at the crabs they'd caught, or throwing balls to them. She often eulogised about them in the evening, pointing out this-one's or that-one's finer traits.

When I was younger, I sometimes thought she loved them more than me. I guess they were all the other sons she never had. I often wondered why they liked her so much. She said it was because she liked them, which didn't make sense given that she thought all males were idiots. She said that the French loved their women *because* of their foibles, not *despite* them and that she loved the boys *because* of their foibles, not *despite* them, and that included me. I vowed to remind her of my admirable 'foibles' the next time she blasted me.

The girl watched the pelicans until they were out of sight, then slowly stood up and walked along the shoreline towards the far end of the caravan park. One pelican that hadn't flown off with the others followed her from a respectable distance, its awkward waddle a contrast to her graceful strides. I wished I could follow from behind, dressed in pelican disguise. I wished I could stop being shy.

Beef

My mother's ability to penetrate the human psyche knew no bounds. From her perspective, all men were idiots. She used to say things like, "The Y chromosome addles the brain" and "Arrogance and ignorance are a powerful cocktail, of which too many people have drunk too deeply."

She used to say a lot of things when we were at Indented Head, as if the sea air cleared the fog between her ears and she understood what life was really about. She kept reminding me and my friends that the secret to life lay in appreciating the ordinary, like fresh tomatoes on toast with a sprinkle of salt and pepper. The kids would come past and say, "Has your Mum had her tomatoes on toast yet? Now can she drive us to the surf beach?"

She kept saying that the closer a person was to their food source, the better it tasted. I remember one time when I entered the Indented Head fishing contest with Aaron, we came back with three squid. We cleaned them and skinned them and cooked them ourselves. I had never tasted anything so good, so sweet and tender. Most of the fishermen around Indented Head, enjoyed eating their own catch. I didn't think it was a particularly profound insight on Mum's part.

One night when she was chomping on a barbecue steak, I asked her whether she could really enjoy eating a steak she hadn't rustled herself. She said she'd only rustled cattle once in her life, and that it was a long time ago. She said that she'd been working for a theatre company based in a little town called Kentucky, just outside Armidale in N.S.W., and this theatre group was run by a French director who used to be a chef. He kept the group running by selling fresh blood sausages and pâté to the restaurants in Sydney.

One day, he told his company of actors that they were running out of money, and he needed a cow. So one night Mum and a few other actors stole into the property next door and started herding cows towards the chef's property. At around midnight they finally got a cow inside the chef's barn, where they watched him bang the beast over the head, slit its throat and drain all its fresh blood into a big stainless-steel tub. Then he got his actors to help him hoist the cow up, with its legs splayed in four directions. They all watched while he slit open its belly and hauled out the entrails. Mum said that nothing smelled quite like death. She walked outside and vomited up her guts. She said that most of the other actors became vegetarians after that.

I told her that one day I wanted to try all the best food from all the best restaurants around the world. She said that one day I'd come back to the simple delights of fresh tomatoes on toast.

The Empty Caravan

The empty caravan was perched high on the cliff top overlooking the wreck. It arrived at the beginning of each summer in the dead of night, and disappeared again in the mists of autumn. People said that it had been coming to the park for over fifty years. No one knew who it belonged to, where it came from, or how it got there. One or two of the oldest campers said that they vaguely remembered a time when it was inhabited by a man and a woman who came each summer with a little boy.

When we were young, we'd spend hours trying to peek through the cracks between the curtains or crawling underneath and pressing our heads up against the floor, listening for footsteps. Sometimes at night, we'd light a campfire down on the sand and fossick for fabrications. We'd tell tales of voodoo and vampires, murder and mayhem, beatings and betrayals, redemption and revenge.

Clancy said that his big brother Jack had broken into the van one year and had found two skeletons locked in each other's arms on the bed. And there was a rank smell that seeped from every crack and crevice that never blew away in the summer squalls. Aaron said the smell came from all the rats that lived in there, surviving off the flesh of the dead bodies left behind after the vampires had sucked them dry.

One year, Clancy burst into our caravan, white as a sheet and shaking. He said he'd heard a woman's voice, soft and sweet, singing 'hush little baby, don't you cry' inside the empty caravan. Me and Clancy scrambled up the cliff and crawled under the van. We listened for ages but I didn't hear anything.

"Shush," said Clancy."

I pressed my ear harder to the bottom of the van, "Nothing," I whispered.

"Shut-up, I heard it," insisted Clancy.

Then I heard it, a woman's voice, softly singing snatches of a song, like it was a long way off, carried on the wind, like it was coming from about three caravans down, where one of the mums had a toddler. I whacked Clancy over the head, "You're a friggin' idiot!" Then he whacked me back, and I cracked my head on the iron chassis that ran under the van. We clambered back down the cliff and went home. Clancy stared at my neck, "What's that?" I wiped my neck and stared at the blood on my hand.

"Nothing, I banged my head on the van."

"Bullshit, she got ya! Ya done for! Ya dead! Ya gonna turn! You're gonna become one of them! You're a friggin' vampire!"

Clancy kept his distance for three whole days, occasionally following me and peering at me from behind caravans. He told all the other kids to keep away from me until he gave them the all clear, 'cos I'd turned.

Another time, we were all just sitting around the campfire staring into the flames, takin' it easy, when Aaron said "Vampires do have red eyes, everyone knows." Bryce stared at his older brother, his eyes popping out of his head.

"That woman I heard singing in the empty caravan is definitely a vampire," said Clancy.

"Soothin' her kids to sleep just before she sucks them dry," I added.

"A girl went missing last year from the playground of the next park down," said Zeke.

"Bet we'd find her skeleton if we broke into the empty van," said Clancy.

"No one's ever broken in. Someone said there's something you've got to say before any key will turn the lock," said Zeth.

We sat in silence concentrating on the flickering flames, figuring out possible codes, as the off shore breeze blew warped words of wisdom from deep within the bowels of the wreck.

"My sister threw a rock at it once and cracked a

window but it didn't smash in. She copped it from Mum for vandalising other people's property," piped up Hope, breaking the silence.

"What do ya have to say to get in," asked Bryce.

"How do I know?" Aaron coughed as smoke from the fire blew his way.

"Maybe there's a clue," I said.

"Like what?" asked Bryce.

"Like the number plate." Clancy nudged Bryce. "Go up and whisper the number plate three times."

Bryce shook his head and inched closer to Aaron but Aaron just shoved him away and told him to get up the cliff before he whacked him one. Bryce inched his way up the cliff, in the dark. After a while we just forgot about him.

"Jack broke in once, said he had sex with a girl, right there on the bed," said Clancy.

"What about the two skeletons?" asked Zeke.

"He said he just shoved them off the bed onto the floor."

"Was the girl a virgin?" asked Zeke.

"How would I know," Clancy shrugged.

"They leave blood the first time."

"Did she leave any blood on the bed," asked Aaron impersonating Sherlock Holmes.

"That mattress would have been covered in blood from all the bodies sucked dry by vampires," said Zed.

"If a vampire sucked them dry, there wouldn't be any blood," I deduced.

Then, Bryce came hurtling down the cliff, smashing through the shrubs. "I said it; the number plate, I said it three times and she stared at me through the crack in the curtains. She's got red eyes."

"I already told ya that, idiot brain," snapped Aaron who was annoyed with his little brother for interrupting the conversation. "How did Jack know what to do?"

"To get in the van?" asked Clancy.

"Nah, to get in the girl," teased Zeth.

"He read the magazines we found that summer a few years ago, up on the secret path between the bushes. Remember? All rolled up and shoved down the snake hole."

"Why did you put your hands down a snake hole?" asked Hope.

"We were looking for snakes."

"What was in the magazines?"

"Stuff, sexy stuff, big boobs."

"Guess Jack learned what to do with his snake," Zeke delivered the punchline.

"HAHAHA," we all laughed.

Bryce wasn't laughing, he was shaking. "It's not funny. She's got red eyes," he repeated his original claim. So we all climbed up the cliff, keeping as low as possible. We stared at the van from behind the bushes. It looked like a giant sleeping dinosaur, dark and still in the moonlight. It was a prehistoric monster on the verge of waking up and hunting for its evening meal. But just as we had mustered enough courage to tiptoe towards it, Ziggy, one of the younger Zees, shoved Bryce crying, "There's nothin' there!" Then Aaron shoved Ziggy for shoving Bryce. I shoved Aaron for shoving Ziggy, and Clancy shoved me for shoving Aaron. We all tumbled in a tangle of limbs down the cliff face.

The fire had nearly burned out, so Zeke shoved another branch on and said that some kid had crawled under the van one time and felt something dripping on his head and down his face. Then he noticed something dripping from the floor; little red drops, dripping from the cracks in the floor, little drops of blood, dripping all over his head. Zeke said he'd heard that there had been an argument between twin brothers about who owned the van. One brother had stabbed the other brother and left his body there to rot, but it didn't rot, and every night at around 10 p.m. the body would start to bleed, because that was the exact time he'd been stabbed.

Grandad

One Christmas I got a kayak, a real one not a kid's one. So, Clancy and I decided to row all the way across the bay to Frankston, which lies directly opposite Indented Head. My grandparents lived in Frankston and Grandad was sick in Frankston hospital.

I liked Grandad. He had a big mop of curly hair like my mother's hair, and he was loud and funny and liked to tell stories, but when he got old, he coughed a lot and made all sorts of strange wheezing and gurgling noises because he had trouble breathing. Mum said that he had emphysema from smoking a pack a day and that he was dying. When I told her that me and Clancy were going to row over and visit him, she laughed and said

"I don't think anyone has ever rowed across the bay and lived to tell the tale." She said that the bay could be a treacherous place, flat one minute and blowing squalls the next. "Good luck, and wear your safety jackets, and make sure you're back for dinner!" She waved us off cheerily. It struck me that my parents were weird. One minute they wouldn't let you row past the wreck, and the next minute they didn't seem to care what you did.

Clancy and I rowed and rowed. I think we almost made it halfway across. From the shoreline at camp, we could see all the way over to the other side of the bay. The outlines of Mt. Eliza and Mt. Martha didn't seem that far away, but as we rowed, they seemed to slip further and further into the distance. After a few hours, with our arms aching and our hands beginning to blister, as we gripped the paddles, we decided to stop for a break to try and figure out the mathematical or magical conundrum of distance. How was it possible to have rowed so far from the shoreline of Indented Head and yet be no closer to Frankston? We decided that it was probably an optical illusion and that we might in fact be closer than we thought, or given that we couldn't see any high-rise buildings, there was the possibility that we hadn't travelled as far as we imagined.

Clancy was all for pushing forward, conquering our fears and the forces of nature. I, on the other hand, listened to the grumbling of my belly, noted the ominous cloud formations overhead and felt the dimming of the light. By the time I had convinced him that it was better to be safe than sorry, and that we should cut our losses and row back to camp, a squall had blown up. The sky went grey, the wind gathered force and big drops of rain started to pelt against our faces. The sea started to swell with big waves that gathered us up into their arms, then dropped us unceremoniously into the dip. As we cried out, our mouths filled with water and our eyes teared up with the salty sting of sea-spray. Our kayak was nothing more than a drop in the ocean. I thought this is it! This is where my story ends! Then I started to think about death. I figured Grandad and I were both thinking about death and that it would be strange if we both died at exactly the same moment. I thought it would be good to have him there by my side in the great unknown, if there was one, if we didn't just disappear into a black void of nothingness. Then, just as I was contemplating a possible afterlife, Clancy screamed, "What the hell are you doing ya friggin' frog wit! Wake up, we're on our way to Tasmania, through The Heads. Yee Ha!"

"Shut up ya moron, we're gonna die! No one survives Bass Strait," I shouted.

"Maybe we'll land halfway, on King Island."

"More likely to end in a shark's stomach!"

"Maybe we should pray," suggested Clancy doubtfully.

"Who to?" I demanded.

"I don't know to some god; the god of the sea."

"Poseidon or Neptune?" I asked, although it wasn't a good time to be splitting hairs.

"I don't know. I don't care. Just do it!"

"Why me?" I questioned his offloading of responsibility. I didn't have a great track record with summoning the masters of the universe.

"You're better with words," reasoned Clancy.

"You're better with fish," I countered.

"Shut-up, just do it!"

So I raised myself up as straight as I could, and yelled above the noise of the storm:

'Poseidon, Neptune!

Gods of the sea

Send a boat to rescue

Clancy and me!

Send it soon

And send it fast

'Cos I dunno how long

This kayak will last!'

We waited. The thunder gave a chesty rumble worse than Grandad's breathing on a bad day and great forks of lightening, like Neptune's trident, pierced the sky.

"See, it's a sign!" screamed Clancy.

We waited and waited, but nothing happened, the waves tossed us up and dumped us down. We were cold and hungry. Some residue sand in my board shorts had created a rash in my groin which stung like hell. Then, just as we were cursing leaving the shore, a weird white sheet of godly glare swept the sky and we heard the coast guard's siren. They picked us up and took us back to the caravan park.

Our parents were waiting on the shore. Clancy's parents waved and cheered as we got out of the boat and hugged Clancy close, saying over and over again that they were glad we were safe. Mum and Dad just stood there, stony-faced; Mum with her hands on her hips and Dad with his arms crossed. It wasn't the warmest of welcomes. Then the tirade began:

"Vhy, vhy vhy must you being a moron? Vhy, vhy, vhy do I try, try, try making you not a moron," my father demanded as he glared at me in disbelief that I'd actually had the gall to return. "Vhy is your mother the moron who lets you go?"

I peered at Mum, hoping that she would at least take half the blame for my transgression, but she just shrugged and said, "Don't look at me. How was I to know you'd actually be silly enough to try and row across the bay. I just thought you'd get tired after an hour and come home, like any normal person! Do you realise you put Clancy's life in danger? Can you imagine how his parents would have felt if he'd drowned? Well?"

There was no point in answering her questions. She obviously cared more about Clancy's life than mine and she obviously believed that I deserved to die! Then just as I was about to disown my parents, Mum wrapped her arms around me and kissed me on the forehead, "I know you're worried about Grandad. I've been thinking we should go over and visit him." Then Dad ruffled my hair with his big rough hand and said, "You think ve veren't vorried about you? Of course, ve vere vorried!

The next morning Mum called the hospital and learned that Grandad wouldn't last much longer, so we drove to Queenscliff and caught the last ferry to Sorrento, then drove to Frankston hospital where we held Grandad's hands all through the night. He kept saying that he was hungry and wanted a nice sizzly sausage, but all the nurse would give him were lumps of ice to suck. Apparently dying people aren't allowed to eat. I told the nurse that even on death row prisoners were allowed to have a final supper, anything they wanted; roast lamb with peas and carrots and roast potatoes, followed by apple pie with custard, anything at all. She said that Frankston Hospital was not death row and that she was not our own private chef, and that it was better to die on an empty stomach. So we watched Grandad slip further and further into unconsciousness, on an empty stomach, until he finally slipped away.

About a week later, at the funeral, Mum delivered Grandad's eulogy. This is what she said:

"I liked my dad. I would have liked him as a person even if he hadn't been my dad. He was smart and funny. He had a big cheerful laugh and a big warm voice with a true-blue Aussie accent, typical of blokes of his generation. He liked to laugh and he liked to make other people laugh. I remember when we were kids, he'd walk down to the local shops to get the newspaper and he'd come home and have us in stitches telling us about who or what he'd seen. He could take something ordinary and make it seem hilarious; like the time he saw our next-door neighbour down at the shops. She was struggling with her shopping and some man stopped to help her, but she thought he was a robber, so she started hitting him over the head with a parcel of sausages. Finally, the paper fell off and the sausages scattered over the footpath and all the dogs in the neighbourhood swooped on them. This made the woman so angry she started hitting the man with a packet of biscuits, until they eventually split open and scattered everywhere. By the time Dad had finished his story, our neighbour didn't have any shopping left to take home, and the man said he was happy to have helped her lighten her load, and all the while a band of cats slurped happily on her spilt milk. I never knew if that story was entirely true, because when I asked the lady next door if she'd dropped her shopping recently, she looked at me strangely and said that she was not in the habit of dropping her shopping!

Dad had a way with words and was an astute observer of human nature. He, more than anyone else, shaped the way I see the world. He infused my childhood with humour and a sharp sense of the absurd. I remember the veggie wars. They started when I was about three. Dad would glare down at me with his steely grey-blue eyes and say, 'Eat ya veggies,' and I'd glare up at him with the same grey-blue eyes and say, 'No!' and clamp my mouth shut. People said Dad and I were a lot alike. The veggie wars raged for years. I remember once he banged the kitchen table with his fist. I remember thinking that if he was going to be like that, I wouldn't eat my chops either. He yelled that children in Africa were starving, so I yelled that he could 'send my veggies to Africa.' 'How are we going to do that?' he demanded. 'In an envelope of course!' I growled. I couldn't believe that he was incapable of figuring out the bloody obvious! Finally, after about three nights of stubborn dispute, Dad who was a union rep, brought his negotiating skills to the kitchen table. We settled on chops and mashed potatoes, and we agreed that veggies didn't taste too bad if they were in a stew.

Work was a big part of Dad's life and he worked hard from the age of twelve until the age of sixty-five. He was a union rep for the printing trade and I think those were some of his happiest years. He loved fighting for better pay and conditions. He felt that he was making a difference, and he loved the world of Trades Hall; the political banter and having a beer and a laugh with his mates. But his sense of equality and fair play wasn't just confined to the workplace, he brought it home with him. He believed that husbands and wives should share the household duties equally. So, Dad cooked the dinner every Monday, Tuesday and Wednesday night, and on Thursdays after work, he did the big weekly shop. He'd come home with boxes of fresh fruit, veggies and meat, and on Sundays, he'd cook the Sunday roast. Those were the days when lamb was cheaper than chicken, so roast chicken was a real treat. I remember when he discovered how to cook 'gourmet roast chicken,' which involved chucking a can of apricots on top of the chook and letting the sweet syrup soak into the meat. Week after week we had this delicious dish until finally, I asked Dad if we could just have a roast chicken without the 'gourmet.'

Dad didn't just cook, he also washed the dishes each night. I know, because he made me dry them. Night after night, year after year, I went kicking and screaming to the kitchen sink. I stood there sulking and drying the dishes, while Dad washed up and tried to make me laugh. It was our time together. He'd say, 'What doesn't come off with the dish cloth comes off with the tea towel,' which later in life I discovered held true for more than just dishes.

When I was a bit older Dad would listen as I wrestled with the dishes and tried to put my thoughts together, attempting to articulate my opinions of whatever issue I thought was important at the time. It didn't matter if it was naïve perceptions of domestic politics, anti-conscription raves, insights into the Vietnam war, or the bewildering behaviour of boys at school. He knew that if a person was going to learn to speak up for themselves, then the best way to learn was to have someone who would listen. I'm always grateful to Dad for listening. He'd always let me finish my train of thought before he offered his own opinions.

Dad never seemed to want more than he had, so I grew up thinking we were rich. Dad was happy to dig in the garden, or to watch his kids playing in the back yard, or to watch the Tigers play footy, or to sit Mum on his knee for a bit of a cuddle. Being content with what he had was Dad's wealth. He wasn't religious, but he had a great appreciation of nature. He took good care of the roses in our front garden and always pointed out the most beautiful blooms, and he'd make sure we knew when the lemon tree had blossomed in spring. He made sure we noticed when the leaves on the Liquid Amber and Silver Birch trees had turned gold in autumn, and he filled our sunroom with orchids, dozens of pots of the most exquisite orchids, every shade of pink and yellow and rare colour combinations that he'd bred himself. It's no wonder my brother became a florist.

In many ways Dad was a homebody. He liked being at home, whether it was in the old house or the new one they moved into when he and Mum moved to Frankston. He was always there, like a still point in the universe, and when Mum and I went on our travels;

me for years in New York and Mum trotting all over the globe, we both knew that Dad would be there when we got back, sitting quietly in his chair by the window, smoking. I always remember him saying, 'Ya don't have to rush around all over the place to know what's going on in the world,' and he always did know what was going on in the world. He read the newspaper every day and listened to the radio, and could argue the ins and outs of international politics better than most.

Dad was pretty tough. He came from a poor family and started work young. He endured the discomforts of emphysema for many years without complaining or seeking sympathy. He had dignity. He loved Mum and his two sons and his grandson and me. Rest in peace Dad and know that you are loved and very much appreciated."

Then Mum read out a poem I'd written for Grandad years ago in year 7, called 'Cardigan Poem:'
Grandad is an earthy brown
He is Saturday's footy replay
He is a big worn-out cardigan
Grandad is a 'barmy' night
He is a traditional roast with extra meat
He is an old radio crackling A.B.C. news
Grandad is an old broken-down Volvo that still
    drives
Although he sometimes explodes like overheated
    Mars
He is still my Grandad and I love him.

It wasn't until I heard my mother's eulogy that I realized

there was a lot to my Grandad that I didn't know. What I also found strange was the fact that Clancy's Pop had died a couple of summers before mine, and his family had had to pack up camp and go home for the funeral. Then many years later my Nan died while we were camping at Indented. I bet if I asked around, I'd discover that lots of grandparents had died while their families were camping. Maybe old people just got lonely over the summer break. Maybe death crept a little closer when families weren't around to wave it away.

When I thought about death, I wondered if anyone in the new girl's family had died. I wondered if that was the reason she seemed so sad and far away.

Perry

My mother told me that Perry was a pirate, at least he used to be. He has a patch over one eye and limps on a steel leg, on account of his real leg being eaten by a shark when he was diving way out in the centre of the bay, near The Heads, one year. Mum used to say that he was once the captain of the Ozone and went down with his ship, then rose again on the third day as protector of the bay. I remember saying that he must be pretty old.

"Why did he rise on the third day," I asked her.

"I don't know. Maybe that's how long it takes to reconstitute," was Mum's answer.

"Reconstitute? Sounds like orange juice. You know, on the bottle, it says, 'reconstituted' orange juice."

"Don't be an idiot," said Mum. "It's not about orange juice, it's about gods. They all seem to die and then come back; like the Egyptian sun god Ra, who died and rose again each morning, and then of course there's Osiris who was chopped into pieces then put back together."

"Like Jesus," I contributed.

"Yeah, he died then popped up again after three days."

"But Perry is not a god, he's a fisherman," I said, trying to get some sense into the conversation.

"So was Jesus. Just goes to show, gods or fishermen, it's a three-day cycle."

"When I was little, you told me Jesus rose again on the third day as the Easter Bunny and I believed you! At school when that kid, Dylan, said you were wrong, I whacked him one. I defended your honour!"

"Well, it would have been nice if Jesus had risen from the dead as the Easter Bunny and had given all the kids Easter eggs."

"I don't think they had chocolate in the Middle East two thousand years ago," I retorted. My mother was becoming more and more nonsensical.

"Yeah, well he would have had to reconstitute somewhere in South America, like Ecuador, where they had cocoa beans!" Mum was grasping at straws.

"You can't just go around changing history, changing major religions!" I protested.

"Why not? Myths and religions are always evolving, shifting like Chinese whispers," Mum insisted, lost in a whirlpool of wacky wisdom.

"The fact remains that Jesus did not come back as the

Easter Bunny! And the Ozone was never a pirate ship! It was a paddle steamer built in Scotland in 1886. It was one of the finest paddle steamers ever built and could hold thousands of passengers. When it was brought out here, as a tourist attraction, it took people on day trips all around the bay for thirty years, and when it got too old, they dismantled it and sunk it at Indented Head as a breakwater."

"Where did you hear all that rubbish?" demanded Mum.

"I read it on the information board, next to the walking track."

"Who reads information boards?"

"Not you, obviously!" I snapped.

"The fact remains, Perry rose again on the third day as protector of the bay!" Mum always had the final say.

Mum stuck to her story. She insisted that one life bleeds into the next with barely a mist in between, just the thin thread of a theme carried from one lifetime to another, and Perry's theme was the sea. Whatever he needed to know would be taught by the sea; a salty insight into human nature.

Sometimes when we were kids and the tide was out, Perry would take us all on a tour through the seagrass and rock pools, pointing out different kinds of crabs, tiny silverfish and all the spiky things that lived there. He'd alert us to the still shape of a Blue-ringed octopus, silently waiting in the warm still waters for fidgety fingers and delving digits. He told us that the Blue-ringed ones were deadly and could kill a person in just a few minutes. We'd stare in awe and tiptoe carefully as we followed him, hanging onto every word. Then the next day, caution would be thrown to the wind as we slid over the sea grass and into the rock pools. We'd lift rocks and ferret for crabs, forgetful of the pools' dark secrets.

The truth was, Perry worked at the Marine Museum, taking people on tours in glass bottomed boats. There was nothing he didn't know about the bay. He recognized every fish and could name each one with precision, as if they were his brothers and sisters and cousins. He would work his way through the alphabet from Australian Bass to Whiting, fearing that if he forgot the name of even one fish, it might disappear, like so many others. It was almost as if a fish's very existence was dependent on his memory. But there were other factors that he couldn't control, like the flow of phosphates out of Werribee sewage processing plant. He said that one year a long time ago, during a storm, so many phosphates flooded the bay that the algae went bananas and spread out like a slimy green blanket, blocking out the sunlight and sucking the oxygen from the water. It destroyed everything below, not just fish but seaweeds and hundreds of brightly coloured flowers which grew in the secret garden, way out in the centre of the bay, not far from where the seals play. Then came the dredging, to make way for bigger and bigger cargo ships. Perry said that the dredging could have killed the bay by stirring up all the lead, arsenic and other poisons that had lurked still and silent on the ocean floor for decades, before industry was regulated. Once the dredging started, the muck spread like an evil cloud, knocking species after species to their knees. It would take years to recover, as the big tankers slid over the surface.

Perry didn't just want to save the bay for the environment's sake, he wanted to save the bay so that he and his mates could fish forever. Perry didn't just love to fish, he loved eating fish. He ate fish for breakfast, lunch and dinner. He'd take his boat out early in the morning and come back with flathead or bream, or whiting, or a nice little gummy shark. Sometimes he'd dive for oysters, or scallops, or mussels, or clams. When he came back, we'd see him hunched over an old ironing board gutting fish, or cracking open oyster-shells. One time he gave me and Bryce an oyster to taste. I rolled it around on my tongue. It was all sweet and salty and watery and rubbery.

"Who needs Viagra?" Perry exclaimed, with a loud chortle.

"What's Viagra?" asked Bryce.

"Niagara, it's better than Niagara. It's a waterfall somewhere," I explained as I attempted to change the subject.

Around dinner time, kids would crowd around Perry's barbecue watching the fresh flathead fillets fry, and now and then he'd toss a piece high into the sky and we'd catch it in our grimy hands, or open our mouths wide and wait for it to fall in. Squawking like a pack of hungry seagulls, we'd fight over a piece of fresh squid. No one cooked squid quite like Perry, all tender and sweet, and covered in a golden batter, lighter than air. Sometimes he'd bring out tin cups of his fish stew and we'd listen in awe as he told us the recipe; the same recipe he'd told us the year before, but we always forgot, so he'd chant it again:

A slurp of olive oil and a chunk of butter
Into the pan and make sure it doesn't splutter
A couple of Snapper cut into chunks
A couple of Whiting chopped into hunks
A nice chopped chilli to make it hot
A handful of green prawns, chuck in the lot
A fistful of scallops to give it more flavour
Add half a cup of whiskey, all the more to savour
Let it all stew for a little while
Then add a handful of parsley for a bit of style

I wanted to take the girl with the silver hair to meet Perry. I felt sure that a good chat with him and a cup of his fish stew would cheer her up. I kept thinking that if she got to know a few more people at the camping ground, she wouldn't be so lonely. I looked around but I couldn't see her anywhere.

The Missing Girl

The park was all whispers and worried looks the summer a little girl went missing from the caravan park next to ours. Mums kept a closer eye on their kids, while dads kept a closer ear on the news, and kids were subject to an 8 p.m. curfew.

Clancy, Aaron, Zeke and I snuck down to the beach after curfew and lit a camp fire. We watched the flames and the smoke twist and twirl. We called out the shapes we saw, the way we used to do with clouds.

"Looks like there's an anchor."

"Nah, it's a seagull. See the wings spread out."

As the flames shifted and changed, I guess we each saw what we wanted to see, our individual psyches or sensibilities projected onto the flames.

"Look!" cried Clancy, "It's like a girl waving!"

"Yeah," I said, "with long red hair blowing around."

"Yeah, I can see her." Zeke agreed.

"Hey, didn't that missing girl have red hair?" asked Aaron.

"Yeah." I stared into the flames and saw a witch's finger beckoning me. I closed my eyes and turned away. "Maybe a kid-eating witch got her."

"Or a vampire," suggested Clancy.

"Or a pedo," piped up Zeke.

"Yeah, it's usually pedos," we all agreed.

We stared into the fire, lost in our own thoughts. The flames took on the shapes of knives dripping blood, and strange long fingers choking a neck.

"She must be scared," said Aaron.

"Yeah," said Zeke. "Little kids are always scared of something. Zadie's always scared of something; sharks, pelicans, plastic bags floating like stingrays in the water. It could have been her, she's the same age."

We all stared into the fire. The hiss and crackle of the wood burning grew louder, more pronounced, like the raspy voice of an old pirate who smoked and drank too much. It sounded raspy like Perry's voice.

"Did ya hear that? What's it saying?"

"Sounds like 'hairs.'"

"Nah, more like 'bears.'"

We listened closely.

"Troll!" yelled Clancy.

"You're a troll!" I whacked him one. "It's 'dolls!'"

A gust of wind swirled the flames into a circle with spokes, so the fire looked like the paddle wheel of the wreck, with red eyes peering through. The eyes turned violet and then green. Perry had green eyes.

"Bears and dolls," the fire hissed.

"Home,' he said 'home'," whispered Aaron.

"'Gnome,' I'm pretty sure he said 'gnome,'" I whispered back.

"Who's 'he'?" whispered Clancy, "And why are we whispering?"

I pointed to the fire. "Him, in there. I think it's Perry."

"He's asleep in his caravan!" insisted Clancy, trying to keep a grip on reality.

"I'm talking about the old him, from back when he was captain of the Ozone, before it sank. Maybe when he's asleep his spirit travels. Maybe he watches over the bay by day and by night. Yesterday he said he saw hundreds of goatfish, red snapper. He said that the squid were breeding again, and that in a few years the big netters will be banned, so there'll be more fish for ordinary blokes with a rod. His spirit glides over the bay at night to make sure the big netters aren't pulling too many fish. His wife said that one morning she woke up to find Perry sound asleep with a big chunk of sea lettuce hanging out of his mouth and strands of Neptune's necklace seaweed strung around his neck. Maybe he knows where the girl is."

"What were the words again?" asked Aaron. "What were they? 'Gnomes, dolls, teddies.'"

I started to laugh. "The old lady's house! Remember, a few streets back, where we used to go when we were little kids. Remember all the dolls and teddies in her front yard?"

"Yeah, and the wishing well!"

"And all the gnomes; the biggest gnome collection I've ever seen."

"And a mirror on the ground for a pond!"

"Yeah, and remember the frog statues: hear no evil, see no evil, speak no evil."

It was true. The old lady that owned the house had never had any children, so she had created a children's garden to entice all the kids into her front yard, so she could chat to them. She'd sit on her front porch in a big straw hat, as still as a statue, so the kids thought she was a scarecrow, then she'd suddenly spring to life and scare the hell out of them. We all loved that place, especially the girls, because there were so many dolls. During the year the old lady would go into Geelong and visit all the op-shops and come back with dozens of dolls. Every year there would be a few new ones that we'd never seen before.

"Maybe she's over there. Maybe the girl is at the old lady's place," said Zeke. "Zadie loves that place. She's always begging Mum to take her over there."

"Worth a try, the old lady might have seen the missing girl. She might know something." said Clancy.

"It's late, she'll be asleep," I said.

"Let's go!" said Zeke.

We kicked sand over the fire, then made our way through the dark back streets behind the general store. When we reached the old lady's house all the lights were out. All the dolls, and bears, and gnomes looked eerie in the moonlight. It felt like they were all staring at us. I pushed Clancy. "Go knock on the door."

Clancy pushed Zeke. "Go on, you do it."

A light wind blew a few leaves across the yard, as the gnomes whispered secrets to each other. Zeke shoved me in front of him just as a cat let out a high-pitched meow and scampered past us, probably on the trail of a rat. Then the curtains covering the windows seemed to move slightly. It was all too much for us big brave boys as we hovered close to each other.

"Her eyes moved!" yelped Zeke pointing to a large doll in a long pink dress, sitting on the cane chair on the porch. "I swear I saw her head move!" Aaron must have seen it too because he bolted back to the caravan park as fast as he could. Me and Clancy and Zeke were hot on his heels. Once we were on safe ground, we decided that it might be best to go visiting in broad daylight, when the nocturnal activities of dolls and gnomes had come to an end.

The next day, we knocked on the old lady's door. She was delighted to see us. "Come in, come in! I'm just making tea. We can have a tea party!" she chortled.

We held our ground. "I don't like tea," said Clancy.

"Cordial then?" offered the old lady.

"Lemonade," bartered Zeke.

"Strawberry milk?" rallied the old lady.

"Chocolate milk," bargained Clancy.

"I think you boys must be lost. You must be looking for the milk bar!"

Clancy elbowed Zeke. "Only girls drink strawberry milk."

"You haven't seen any girls around, have you?" asked Zeke.

At that moment a little girl scurried out from behind the old lady. "She's got lots of strawberry milk and lots of dolls!" It was Zadie. Zeke was fast. He reached through the doorway and grabbed her hand, then hurled her onto his back and ran. Zadie giggled, "Giddy-up horsey!"

"Come back!" cried the old lady, "I've got lots more dolls to show you!"

We took Zadie back to the Zees' caravan, where Zeke's mum said that she had been worried sick, and told Zadie not to wander off by herself again. She said that she had been looking for Zadie all morning, and wanted to know how we knew where she was. We just shrugged. We all silently agreed that it probably wasn't worth mentioning that we had heard Perry's voice in the fire the night before.

Later that day as we dangled our feet off the wreck, we wondered what could have happened to the missing girl. We all agreed that she probably wasn't at the old lady's house, and we all agreed that bad men did bad things to little kids. We sat in silence for a long time, each of us lost in our own hellish imaginings.

The next summer, we noticed that all the dolls and bears and gnomes were gone from the yard of the old lady's house. Instead, there was just a big FOR SALE sign out the front.

Zachariah

Zeke's dad was called Zachariah. He was a minister and a surfie. We all found it strange. Who would have thought ministers went surfing or camping? Most of us imagined ministers just spent all day hanging around in churches.

When he was young, Zachariah did not want to follow in the footsteps of his father and become a minister, so he became a foreman in a factory. He had a way with numbers. He knew where things were or where they should be, and if they weren't there, he knew where to find them. He had an easy manner which put others at ease. People liked working with him. He had practical skills and a good head on his shoulders.

Zachariah met his future wife, Zoe, in a pub when he was out having a counter dinner with a mate. She sat at the next table with a friend. She had blonde hair, the brightest, bluest eyes, and she kept flashing him the sweetest, pearliest smile. He watched her eat a double serve of ribs. She seemed like the kind of girl whose heart was as big as her appetite. He invited her to dinner the following night and watched her eat a double serve of Surf and Turf. He liked her appetite. He liked her generosity of spirit. He liked the way she laughed. After they had been going out for a while, they got married and set up house in Geelong, where they embarked upon the creation of the Mighty Zees.

The problem was, Geelong wasn't much of a place for jobs. It had been gutted when a number of companies had closed down, and even a man with Zachariah's skills found it hard to keep regular work. So one day, Zachariah knelt and prayed, and asked God what He wanted him to do, and in that moment, just as a ray of sunlight played upon Zachariah's temple, it became crystal clear that he could not avoid his fate; just as electricians breed electricians, just as teachers breed teachers, just as carpenters breed carpenters, so ministers breed ministers. There was no escaping the force of his lineage. So he and Zoe decided that the best thing for him to do would be to go to theology school, then become ordained.

It took a few years but he finally made it through and was given a surfside flock to attend. It was a parish full of wet suited water lovers, fisherman and fish wives. He felt perfectly at home there, and never felt the need to cut his hair or change his board shorts.

When he told his surfie mates that he had become a minister, they scattered in all directions, mistrustful of his mission, feeling betrayed, wary of his judgement. Regardless, he returned to the beach each morning when the surf was up. He paddled out with the rest of them; each one silently worshipping at the altar of almighty Poseidon, whispering their humility in the face of his liquid grandeur, silently praying, patiently waiting for the perfect swell, the perfect drop, and the longest ride deep within the rip curl, the heart of liquid glass.

Zoe, whose father was a baker, hoped to create a baker's dozen worth of Zees. She dreamed of having twelve kids and an extra one for luck. Each summer that we camped at Indented Head, there seemed to be an extra Zee wandering about. They were indeed, 'The Mighty Zees', each one a blonde-haired, blue-eyed Adonis or Athena, born with high arched feet for running, strong calves, broad shoulders, slim waists and barrel chests. Each one was an athlete in his or her own right: Zekiel ran faster than a panther, Zara could out row her brothers in any kayak challenge, Zedekiah, kicked a footy further than any A.F.L. player, Zebedee swam faster than a shark, Zeth climbed like a mountain goat, Zoltan could wrestle like a bear, Zavier rode his bike faster than a cyclist in the Tour de France, Ziggy dived deeper than a dugong, and Zadie was hero at hopscotch. Some of the Zees had names drawn from the bible but when Zachariah's faith began to fail him, he spread his naming net far and wide and found inspiration in the 'Babies' Names Guide' book.

At night as he lay with his head on Zoe's breast and felt it rise and fall, he matched his breathing to hers and drifted in sleepy reverie; afloat on his board, stretched out with the sun on his back, drifting on the gentle swell between breakers on a slow surf day, and he wondered if Jesus hadn't made a terrible mistake in not marrying his Magdelana.

The End Is Nigh

One summer, I remember the Zees piling out of the family's mini-bus. They had just returned from Zachariah's Sunday sermon. Zeke said that for the past year his father had mostly lectured the congregation on the degradation of the environment rather than the degradation of man's morals. Zachariah felt that bushfires were more pressing than fire and brimstone, and he was more worried about the evils of plastics than the evil in men's hearts.

The Great Pacific garbage patch, an island of plastic the size of the U.S., was often the focus of his sermons. For him it represented the beginning of the end. He'd show videos of seagulls, dolphins, turtles and penguins dead on seashores with their bellies split open, engorged with plastic bottle tops, broken plastic toys, plastic straws and plastic bags. Zachariah formed his congregation into beach patrols to rid God's shores of plastics and cigarette butts. His children were his own private environmental army.

One particular Sunday, his eyes ablaze, his spirit whipped into a frenzy of righteous indignation, Zachariah vowed to clear every piece of plastic from Indented Head to Portarlington. He called upon the rest of us to join the long march, and handed out cotton pillow cases to hold the rubbish. We walked in a horizontal line beside him, sweeping the breadth of the sand. He held up clear squid tubes and sun-bleached sea lettuce and cried, "See how they look just like plastic! How can God's poor creatures know the difference?" He shouted that he had heard of the birth of a white whale, and that he had heard of the birth of a white dolphin, and that the corals of the world were turning white. "When the creatures of the sea turn white, the prophesy has come! The end is nigh! The end is nigh!" As he strode along the shoreline his eyes were ablaze and he chanted:

> "The bellies of the fish swell with man's refuse. The end is nigh!"

And we chorused back "The end is nigh!"

> "The bellies of seabirds swell with man's negligence. The end is nigh!"

"The end is nigh!" we echoed.

> "Dolphins spew the detritus of man's greed. The end is nigh!"

"The end is nigh!" we chanted.

We were about half way to Portarlington when we saw it; a long multi-humped creature, like the Loch Ness monster, floating just off shore. Zachariah stopped and stared. "The black serpent from the lower depths has risen! The end is nigh!" I tried to interject and explain that we were in the area where the black swans congregate. I'd seen it before. The swans would form a single file, each with its head bent beneath the tail feathers of the one in front, their curved necks forming the shape of a long, humped snake-like creature, as they searched for food. Only the swan at the front kept its head above the waterline.

"It's just swans." I called out.

"It's a sign!" cried Zachariah and chanted; "Temperatures are rising. The end is nigh! The seas are warming. The end is nigh! The seas are rising. Retreat! The glaciers are melting. Retreat! Retreat!"

At that moment, in unison, the swans lifted their heads out of the water and turned to stare at us. A black feather floating on the surface, was picked up by the wind and blew into Zachariah's mouth. He began to speak strange words in strange tongues, or perhaps just colourful expletives we'd never heard before. We all stared in awe. I could see that a few of the younger kids were becoming frightened. I tried to diffuse the situation by singing a Christmas carol I'd heard at Carols by Candlelight that year. Instead of 'Deck the Halls with Boughs of Holly' they sang 'Deck the Roofs with Solar Panels, tralalala, lalalala. Zeke's father turned and glowered at me: "Do you mock me son?" he bellowed.

"No, I heard it at Carols by Candlelight," I stuttered.

"Where?" he demanded.

"Northcote."

"And what would the good people of Northcote know about the perils of the shoreline? They're inlanders! Landlubbers!" I tried to remind him that Northcote was only ten kilometres from the shoreline of Port Melbourne, but Zachariah looked right through me and intoned: "From Port Fairy to Mallacoota the high tides devour our shorelines as the creatures of the sea devour our refuse, falling prey to our porcine preoccupations and our failed peripheral vision. The end is nigh!"

I caught Zeke's eye. He just shrugged and started walking back to camp. We all followed, lugging our plastic booty in our cotton sacks. "What's nigh?" asked Bryce.

"It's just an old-fashioned word for near," I answered.

"The end of what?" asked Bryce.

"I guess Zachariah means the end of everything." I answered.

"Oh," sighed Bryce.

I saw silent tears roll down his face as we walked. "It's okay mate, they're gonna ban plastic bags in all the shops," I said clutching at straws. "And they're turning car tyres into building materials. Everything is gonna be recycled. Everyone is gonna put solar panels on their roofs. Everyone is gonna stop being greedy. Everything will get better. We'll do something. We'll think of something."

"How do you know?" asked Bryce.

"Zachariah doesn't know everything. He might still have a bit of faith in God but he's lost faith in humanity. Don't worry Bryce, we'll think of something."

Zachariah and Perry Walk

Zachariah and Perry were friends. It was a natural friendship from the perspective of the environment, but an unnatural friendship from a cosmological standpoint.

In the evenings, in the soft light of sunset, with a gentle breeze blowing off-shore, they'd stroll along the path which runs from the caravan park to the jetty. With beer stubbies in hand and speaking in conspiratorial tones, they'd chew over the details of the degradation and disrespect that was destroying their beach, their fishing grounds. On other occasions, they'd walk further apart, their voices raised as they argued the very nature of man's existence.

Perry held firm to the belief that every man was a god in his own right. He was sure that deep within the cells of every human body was an instinctive memory of all that had ever been; a memory that stretched beyond the beginning of time. He argued that the human spirit was a portion of the whole pulsating conundrum of existence; life in its uninterrupted dynamic. He said that man's knowledge of himself was a profoundly private secret, passed on from one lifetime to the next. Whereas, Zachariah argued that no man could fully know himself or his spirit without the roadmap of religion, which he referred to as, "The collective repository of incremental spiritual insights gathered and recorded over time." He was adamant that mankind was limited in perception and needed intermediaries to facilitate spiritual insight, and that to refer to oneself as a god was blasphemy! Perry agreed that it was probably not a good idea for a person to call himself a god in public, but what he thought in the privacy of his own mind, was his own bloody business! And Perry the pirate was always careful not to mention his own miraculous incarnation.

Sometimes it seemed as if Zachariah was looking for Perry to talk him out of his faith, to debunk the ancient story. He vaguely remembered hearing that there was once a pope who said, "Let us not forget how profitable this myth of Jesus has been." Zachariah wanted Perry to explain why kids were starving in Africa, why children were being bombed in war zones, why God allowed atrocities to happen to the innocent.

There were certain nights when the west wind howled

across the caravan park and he lay in his bed listening to the canvas annex pound against the objects inside, that he hated his God for allowing the worst things to happen. In his mind's eye he saw little kids with their arms and legs and blown off; in places where self-righteous men fought self-righteous causes. He turned the phrase, 'All's fair in love and war' over in his mind, and finally comforted himself with the knowledge that all is not 'fair' and that the rules of war exist. He promised himself that he would read the Geneva Convention when he got back home. But nothing in him could reconcile with the perspective that all the world's evil was due to God's greatest gift to humanity; free will. He tossed and turned and tried to believe in a merciful God who took over the reins when man lost control. The truth was he felt helpless and couldn't see how he could help others when he couldn't even help himself, and being responsible for so many children of his own was sometimes a bit of a strain, both mentally and financially. He worried about how he would support them all if he left the generosity of the church.

When he confessed his doubts to Perry, the wise old sea captain just shrugged and said, "Don't worry mate, it's all a matter of balance; light and dark, good and bad. Ya can't have one without the other." He said that there was no point being kind if there was no one to be kind to, no bravery without a challenge and no loyalty without understanding betrayal. Zachariah nodded but he remained unconvinced. His only consolation was that he would get up early in the morning and go surfing.

I used to wonder how either of them could get back

into the water, given that they had both had near-death experiences there. Perry nearly bled to death when a shark took his leg off one time when he was diving, and he always said that he only survived because his mates acted fast and hauled him back on board the boat in record time, then got him to hospital. The whole experience deepened his faith in humanity. So when Zachariah suggested that it may have been the hand of God that saved him, Perry just shrugged and said, "Bullshit mate, bloody bullshit." In contrast, when Zachariah was out riding the big surf at Bells Beach one time and was seriously dumped and almost drowned, there was no one around to save him. When his ankle strap snapped and the force of the wave dragged him deeper, he prepared to meet his maker, and prayed for someone to take care of his family. And to this day he still doesn't know how he made it to shore, but he believes the Almighty might have had a hand in it.

As for me, I wondered if the girl with the silver hair had ever been surfing. She sort of looked like a surfer girl, like the ones you see in surfie movies, but she didn't act like one. Maybe she'd had some sort of near-death experience that she was trying to come to terms with. I wondered what she thought about the meaning of life. I wanted to talk to her, I wanted to understand what she understood, but the sad part was, I didn't even know her name.

Reflections

Sometimes on grey days, I would walk alone for hours. I'd walk all the way to Portarlington and sit alone high on the hill overlooking the harbour, and if I was still enough and the world was quiet enough, I could feel the space between the protons, electrons and neutrons expanding in my body. Sometimes the nothingness expanded so much that I felt as if I had disappeared. I would run back to the caravan. I'd run all the way back home and when I got there, I'd guzzle mug after mug of water.

"What's wrong?" Mum would ask.

"I was all alone, and I think I disappeared."

"People's sense of reality is anchored in their interaction with others. Go outside and play with the other kids."

"I'm not a kid."

"Who cares. Go outside and play!"

The New Girl

One night, during that summer, the summer I wanted to talk about, that special summer; me and Clancy stepped silently through the shallows on a still night, while Aaron stalked a flounder a few paces ahead.

"Have you seen her?" whispered Clancy.

"Who? Who?" I hooted.

"Quit the owl impersonation. You know who I mean."

"The girl with the silver hair. Yeah, everyone's seen her; you, Zeke, Aaron, Bryce, everyone."

"She's different, she doesn't talk," said Clancy.

"She talks to Bryce."

"That doesn't count, he's only eight, he doesn't feel anything."

"Bullshit, eight-year-olds feel things. All you feel is your pig-headed penis."

"Shut up dick-brain. I like her."

"So what? So does Zeke, so does Aaron. He left a nice bit of squid outside her caravan last night. Maybe you could leave her a pike or a penis fish," I taunted him.

"And what would you leave her?"

I tried to think of something rare and special, "A sea-horse or a sea-dragon. Have you ever seen them float? They're perfectly still."

"They're protected."

"Maybe she's protected. Maybe no one can have her. She seems sort of other-worldly, ethereal."

"Ethereal? Do you have to use friggin' words like 'ethereal'?" Clancy mimicked me in a phoney posh accent.

"Can't help it. When I was three, Mum said I woke her up really early one morning and dragged her out of bed to the lounge room where I'd scattered all my toys and blocks and Lego. Then, with a grand gesture, I pointed to the mess and said 'pandemonium!'"

"So, all you're saying is, you've been a verbal wanker since you were three! I'll tell you who is 'ethereal,' Aaron's mum. I reckon she slipped through some portal. Have you ever noticed how she goes out fishing every morning at about four o'clock and comes back covered in scales? I mean you get a few scales over you when you're cleaning fish, but not like that. I've seen her shimmering all over at sunrise."

"Aaron said she told him that she used to be a mermaid, until his dad caught her when he was out fishing and hooked her right through the cheek. She's got that little scar on the side of her face. By the time he got the hook out, she'd fallen for him. He sweet-talked her until she agreed to come ashore."

"There's gotta be more than one mermaid in the world," pondered Clancy.

"The fact is, no one in that family ever comes back empty handed. They always come back with the biggest catch."

"Yeah, there's something fishy about that family."

"I'd still like to give her a sea-horse."

"Who Aaron's mum?" Clancy, knew I meant the girl with the silver hair. "Like I said they're protected."

"I'd like to protect her. She looks like she needs protection."

"You couldn't protect your big toe. You can't even thread a fishing line. If you were on a desert island you'd starve. You've got no practical knowledge, no practical skills. All you do is read. These days I practically have to beg you to come out floundering at night."

"Yeah, a sea-horse. I'd like to give her a sea-horse, something special."

"I bet she'd rather have something she could eat. What's Zeke giving her?" asked Clancy.

"A taste of his torso. All he does is parade past her with his shirt off."

"Zeke might not get her, but one of the Zees will. They're all golden like her. Like attracts like," pronounced Clancy.

"What about opposites attracting? Maybe she finds our dull brown eyes and our dull brown hair attractive."

"I'm losing confidence by the minute."

"Hey what about that movie, 'A Beautiful Mind'?" I said, raising what I thought was a helpful analogy.

"How's she supposed to know I've got a beautiful

mind?" asked Clancy, who'd obviously missed the point.

"Not your mind dick-brain, that mathematician in the movie. He figured out that if no one went for the blonde, then they'd all get a brunette."

"So, no one gets what they want," stated Clancy, the eternal pragmatist.

"Maybe those guys in the movie didn't know what they wanted, or maybe getting something is better than getting nothing."

"Bullshit! Sometimes ya catch a toady and you throw it back because it's the same as catching nothing, 'cos ya just don't want it!"

We tilted our heads down and resumed the hunt, our small headlamps casting just enough light to make out the shapes flitting over our feet. Aaron was way ahead of us. He always said our chatter scared the fish away and that silence was the key to a good catch, not that Aaron's advice deterred Clancy from holding forth on any topic that interested him at any given point in time, or from yelping with glee when he spotted a flounder. "Got one!" he yelled as he thrust his spear in the general direction of my foot, and in the effort to avoid it, I toppled into the water just as a stingray glided past at chest level, which made me think of that guy Steve Irwin dying with a stingray's barb in his chest. "Shit, missed it! Ya friggin' foot was in the way!" Clancy grumbled.

"Got one!" shouted Aaron holding a flounder high above his head on the end of his spear.

"Aaron's caught a flounder." I stated the obvious.

"Yeah, there's something fishy about that family."

Gilly

She was new. Hardly anyone new ever came to the caravan park. Once a family got a site they held onto it, passing it down from generation to generation. Some caravan sites had been held in the same family for over fifty years, especially the absolute beachfront sites like ours, where there was nothing in front of you except sea and sand and sky.

Everyone noticed her, especially the guys. She was taller than most of the other girls, and slim, and she had a face like an elf, and long silver hair. It wasn't just blonde, it was silver, almost grey, like she'd grown old too soon. I sometimes passed her on the way to the shower block. She kept her eyes down; she didn't look at anybody. She didn't talk to anybody. Mostly she just stood on the shore and stared out to sea. I would watch her from our caravan. I'd never seen anybody be so still for so long. Then every now and then, she'd just dive into the water and disappear for the longest time, then resurface way out from shore. I'd watch while the other guys tried their luck. One day Zeke wandered up, dragging his kayak. I guessed he offered her a ride. She didn't even turn her head, just shook it slightly. Zeke paddled out alone, bare chested, his biceps and back muscles flexing as he paddled. It must have been hard for a girl to resist.

At night, around the camp fire, we'd talk about the new girl and make wild guesses about who she was, and what she was thinking about. She must have been thinking about something. No one even knew her name.

"Maybe she's thinking about year 12. Maybe she failed her exams," suggested Clancy, shifting to avoid a drift of smoke.

"Maybe she's at Uni. She looks kind of mature. I fancy an older woman," Zeke mused, as he rolled his neck and shoulders to loosen a bit of tension.

"Shut up dickhead. No one mature is going to go for a muscle-bound moron like you," taunted Aaron, jabbing the fire with a stick, and we all watched the sparks fly skyward.

"He's not a moron, he's my brother," objected Zeb and kicked sand into Aaron's face. Aaron got him in a pretend stranglehold and held him down for a while as he kicked and screamed. Eventually he calmed down and the soft rhythm of the waves rolling onto shore soothed us all into a contemplative silence.

"Maybe she's worried about something," said Bryce as he stared into the fire with his brows knitted together, trying to figure things out. We all stared at him. This kid was deep.

'Out of the mouths of babes,' I thought. "Maybe she's not thinking about anything. Maybe she's just seeing and feeling everything. You know, like the way you feel when you dive deep down under the wreck. Maybe it's like that, only she does it on land." I said as the breeze shifted and blew smoke into my eyes.

"But she does it for hours."

"Bryce, I've seen you snorkel for three hours straight, just you and the fish and nothing else in your head."

"I bet she's thinking about fish," Aaron concluded, and stood up to gather a few more dry branches from the bushes at the bottom of the cliff.

I rolled my eyes, "I don't think so."

"She could be. Sometimes I stand on the shore like that, trying to figure out what the winds are doing, or how the currents are running, or when the tide will change, or what kind of fish might be out there, that kind of stuff. Maybe she wishes she had a boat. I can't see any boat near her caravan. Maybe her dad doesn't have a boat." Aaron fed the branches into fire.

"Maybe she doesn't have a dad," pondered Clancy.

"Yeah," said Bryce, "Maybe her parents got divorced."

"Maybe I'll ask her if she wants to come out fishing on our boat," said Aaron, "Oh yeah, I forgot to tell you, I found out her name."

The waves stopped rolling, the flames of the fire froze in mid-flight and we all stared at Aaron; his face glinting with golden pride. He said nothing, just stared into the flames, building the suspense and his own self-importance. We waited. He waited for us to break. Silence reigned.

"Okay, enough! What's her name? What is it?" Zeke cracked.

"Gilly, her name's Gilly."

I roared with laughter, "Jilly, you mean Jilly as in Jillian."

"No, I mean Gilly with a 'G,' as in the gills of a fish. My Gilly. I left some nice fresh squid on a plate outside her caravan last night. Maybe she'll take the bait."

The next day, I saw Aaron standing on the shore talking to the girl. I thought it was the perfect time to go over and introduced myself, since Aaron had already broken the ice. I leapt onto the sand and ran into the shallows, stubbed my toe on a rock and sucked up the pain, acting like nothing had happened. "Hi."

Aaron pretended he didn't see me. "What fish is most likely to get into heaven?" he asked the girl.

"I don't know," she said, as she stared at the sea foam caressing her feet.

"An angel fish," I interjected. The girl lifted her head and smiled. It was the first time I'd seen her eyes; they were greyish green like the sea on a cloudy day, and there was something in her gaze that was steady and direct, something that told me she wasn't a fragile elf. Aaron silently mouthed, "Piss off."

"What fish lives at the zoo?" I asked. The girl smiled and shrugged.

"A Zebra fish," snarled Aaron. "What fish plays in a

band?" he challenged me.

Quick as a flash, I answered "A banjo-shark." Aaron and I were into our old routine.

Then Aaron smirked, "What fish looks like Jesse?"

"I wonder?" said the girl, looking right through me. I got the feeling she didn't really care what fish I looked like.

"A flathead," said Aaron laughing his head off.

Then in a fit of utter immaturity I asked, "What fish looks like Aaron?" The girl shook her head. I paused for affect and smiled, "A fat-head."

The girl looked at her feet, embarrassed, then just slipped away, silent as an eel in the shallows on a summer night.

Nose Rings

That summer, half the guys turned up with nose rings. They'd dive deep down under the wreck and come up laughing, their skin all golden and tanned and shimmering in the sun. They'd blow the salty water out of their noses and cling to the rusty side of the wreck, grinning with great green snot-balls hanging from their noses, and the girls laughed, as they balanced on the hull of the wreck; their long skinny golden legs dangling in the water. Miranda, Clancy's sister and Zara were usually there with a few of the Westie girls and after a while Gilly had started to hang-out on the wreck with them. The girls squealed in horror at the surreptitious snot and the boys were thinking it was with pleasure at the sight of their bronzed biceps. Then the boys would face each other and roar with laughter at the grotesque green slime decorating their faces, and as they eyed off the girls' soft pink lips, they thought twice about getting lip rings. They imagined tongues caught and lips torn, and metal meddling with the watermelon taste of melting mouths. Slowly but surely, consciousness crawled into existence.

Aaron had heard that girls found nose rings sexy, so he and his younger brother Lachie had snuck off early one morning and caught the bus into Geelong. They came back in the afternoon, sporting shiny new nose-rings. I was sitting high up on the vertical wheel of the wreck, while Gilly dangled her feet down below on what was left of the other paddle wheel that had collapsed long ago. Aaron swam towards us, waving and shouting, then dived from one side of the wreck to the other, blew his nose and there it was, all green and wormy, caught in the ring. He smiled up at Gilly and she laughed so hard she toppled off the side. I thought of diving in and rescuing her, but I did nothing as usual. I guessed that someone who looked like a mermaid could probably swim. I yelled down to Aaron "Check your ring." He pulled the green worm from its anchor and held it up.

"Might catch something with it," he called.

"Yeah, maybe a whiting," yelled Lachie who'd swam out to meet us.

"Nah, more like a toady."

"Whatever you catch it won't be a girl."

I glimpsed a flash of silver emerging on the shore.

Years later Lachie gave up wearing nose rings and got

a tattoo instead. It was the most majestic tattoo I'd ever seen. It wasn't a paddle steamer like the Ozone, it was an Eighteenth-Century tall ship with four levels of sails that spanned the length of his left arm. It wasn't dyed in lots of colours like some tattoos, it was done in faded blues and greens under a grey wash, as if that great ship were sailing out of an ocean fog after circumnavigating the world. It was a few years later that Lachie became a professional boxer and the wind in the sails behind his left hook left many of his opponents unconscious.

I used to wonder why someone as good as looking as Lachie wanted to risk getting his face punched in when he could have been a model. I remembered seeing a documentary about the great Mohammed Ali, when he was young. He talked about how handsome he was and he said the famous lines, "Dance like a butterfly, sting like a bee." I guess he thought no one would ever get close enough to destroy his good looks. Maybe Lachie thought he was like that, maybe he thought no one would get close enough to do any real damage.

When I glimpsed that flash of silver emerging on the shore, I thought of following her, but instead I dived deep down and swam into the murky depths of the wreck's hull, where great strands of bronze leathery seaweed pawed at my skin like witches' claws, trying to pull me down deeper into their magic. I swam through velvety emerald green tendrils, the soft caresses of sirens fingers luring me deeper, past dark unexplored caverns and over the backs of stingrays sleeping on the sea floor. I felt my stomach knot with fear of some unknown evil lurking in the depths. The tendrils tangled around my ankles and I drifted into the parallel world of the dark web, my home away from home back in the city, where psychopaths spruiked their wares and unhinged war lords traded wise cracks, where chat rooms and crypto kings cracked their heads against the old financial system, screaming for a new one percent. Chan chats chasing Chinamen through a web of Alibaba specials. Alibaba and the new forty thieves treading light footed over crypto dreams. City slickers on the cusp of a new gold rush; every banker's nightmare; ditch the dime for a new fiscal paradigm; crypto cowboys bootlegging invisible dollar bills, looking for virtue in a virtual store of value.

As I drifted into unconsciousness, I felt an arm around my neck and my foot slipped free of the tendrils as Clancy hauled me to the surface. I gasped for air.

"What were you doing down there ya fuckin' idiot. Ya nearly drowned!"

The Mystery Solved

One night that summer, as we sat around the fire, staring up the cliff face to the empty caravan and elaborating on all the stories we'd told the year before, Zeke turned up holding his guitar in one hand and guiding Gilly with the other. He strummed his guitar while Jack swore that the two skeletons he'd seen on the bed a couple of years before, were real. He said he'd heard that they belonged to a man and a woman who had met at Indented Head when they were kids; "Every summer, they collected crabs together in the rock pools when the tide was out, until eventually they fell in love and got married. Then they brought their kids and grandkids down every year, and when they grew old and sick, they made a death pact. They swallowed a heap of sleeping pills and laid down on the caravan bed in each other's arms and waited for death."

"Bullshit," said Zeke, "Dad found out what really happened. He was speaking to the man in the caravan opposite. The man told him that he'd been there when the empty caravan arrived just after sunrise, on the first of December. He said that the van was set up by a man with long grey hair in a ponytail and he had tattoos up his arms. He wore a black, bikie jacket and faded blue jeans. He pulled out a steel stringed guitar from an old battered guitar case and started playing the blues."

Then Zeke started playing his guitar, all soft and slow and sexy. He smiled at Gilly and she smiled back. I scowled into the fire as Zeke continued, "Then the guy started to sing some old song." Zeke started to sing and the girl with the silver hair joined in. All I could think was: 'How come they both know all the verses while I can only remember the chorus, from some old C.D. Mum used to play?' Zeke continued his story: "Apparently 'Stand by Me' was his parents' favourite song and he played it as a tribute to them every year, when he parked their caravan."

"How come he never stayed in it?" asked Aaron.

"He did, when he was a kid, with his parents, but when they got old and died, he just parked it there to honour them and as a way of remembering all the fun he'd had as a kid; snorkelling around the wreck, climbing the cliff, and making a secret path in the scrub, and sitting around the camp fire at night telling ghost stories with his mates." Zeke finished off the final riff with a flourish. The girl laughed with appreciation. "It's the truth, the dead set truth. Dad told me."

"What makes you think it isn't just another story?" I asked.

"He's a minister."

"And ministers don't lie?"

"No, not if they don't have to."

"Like all those pedo priests."

"They're Catholic. My dad's not Catholic."

"What about the Anglicans?"

"What's a pedo?" We all stared at Bryce.

"Shut-up Bryce," said Aaron and Clancy and me, all at once.

"But what's a pedo?" Bryce persisted.

"I meant to say torpedo."

Zeke glared at me. "Yeah, Jesse meant to say torpedo like on a submarine."

"Was your dad in the war Zeke?"

"Nah, he was just talking to old Harry."

Bryce shook his head. "Harry wasn't in a submarine, he was in the jungle, crawling on his belly, that's what he said."

Aaron yanked Bryce to his feet. "Tides out, let's go floundering."

Bryce looked eagerly at me and Zeke, "You wanna come?"

The girl with the silver hair stood up. "I'll come." She looked at me and Zeke in disgust, "Those two have probably done enough 'floundering' for one night."

A New York Story

The summer that Gilly came to the park, it rained for days. Kids crowded into our annex to play board games like Monopoly or Cluedo, or sometimes we played Charades. Mum kept everyone well supplied with cheese and tomato toasties, and when everyone got bored, she'd bring out a big bowl of lollies and launch into one of her New York stories. I'd heard most of them before but that summer she pulled out a few new ones. There was no doubting the fact that Mum loved the sound of her own voice.

One afternoon just as she was about to start, Clancy pushed open the flap of our annex, brushed the wet hair out of his eyes and ushered Gilly inside. I smiled at her and eye-balled Clancy. He just gave me some kind of

Mona Lisa smirk and acted like nothing was out of the ordinary He must have gone over to Gilly's caravan to get her. I kicked myself for not going over and asking her myself. Why was I such a wimp? Why was I so scared of rejection?

Meanwhile, Mum seemed oblivious to the newcomer and just kept prattling on: "I lived in New York City for seven fabulous years. Sure, I came back to Melbourne from time to time to get a new show together, or to do a bit of teaching to make extra money, but mostly I was in New York. When I first got there, I lived in a big loft; a whole floor of an old factory building in Soho, that belonged to a performance artist. She was quite famous in the art scene. Her loft was on Mercer Street, just near Wooster Street. I performed in one of her shows based on Icelandic mythology. Well, the show ended up moving to the Museum of Modern Art for a day, then went to The Whitney for a day."

Mum stared at the kids and deduced that they had no idea what she was talking about, so attempted to explain: "It was performance art, somewhere between theatre, video and living sculpture."

The kids didn't care, they were there for the lollies and they seemed to be indulging in a bit of performance art themselves, as they furtively competed to stuff as many lollies as they could into their mouths.

"This performance artist said that she wanted to use me as an actor in the show because she thought my Aussie accent was strange and exotic, but Icelandic it aint! After that I lived on Greenwich Street for a few years, just near De Niro's bar and grill, you must know who I mean, the actor, Robert De Niro, you've seen him in lots of movies." The kids shrugged and started jostling each other. Mum was getting boring but she continued on:

"The place was a big loft and four of us lived there; me, big El, who was a theatre director, and Tom and Bethany who were film makers. Tom was always making crackpot short films and obsessing about a big project he wanted to film about Pine Gap, which he never made. You know Pine Gap, the secret U.S. military base that everybody knew about, in the desert outside Alice Springs, where they used to control spy satellites. There were always spies creeping around there."

"And what did the spies wear? Black woollen balaclavas in forty-degree heat?" I interrupted, trying to inject a little humour into the situation. I thought that my razor-sharp wit might shift Gilly's attention away from Clancy and more in my direction.

"Don't be silly," Mum retorted. "They probably wore orange army fatigues with a nice yellow sun hat, so they blended into the orange sands of the Aussie desert."

"And what did they do all day? Just lie prostrate like snakes in the grass?"

"Quite possibly, who knows? Apparently being a spy can be quite dull at times," Mum replied, unruffled by my interjections.

"And did they bring a packed lunch?" I asked sarcastically.

"Well of course they did, there aren't any shops out there you know."

"And where did these spies come from?" I tested her.

"Let me think; well, they probably came from China, they've always got spies hanging about, and of course Russia, they've always had spies everywhere, and of course America."

"So, the Americans were spying on themselves, were they?" I challenged her.

"Well of course they were; the C.I.A. is always spying on the F.B.I., and the F.B.I. is always spying on the C.I.A. I saw it on a documentary on the telly."

"On the telly! Oh well then, it must be true!" I cemented my sarcasm.

"It wasn't just on the telly; it was on the A.B.C."

My mother never questioned anything she saw on the A.B.C. and once she had pronounced the first three letters of the alphabet, all discussion ceased.

"Now stop interrupting my story." Mum demanded. "Where was I? Ah, now I remember: Anyway, I guess Tom was ahead of his time. There were always artists, attractive wannabe actors and famous film directors, wandering in and out of our loft. Bethany, who owned the place, seemed to know just about everybody, who was anybody, in New York City. The loft was a whole floor of an old, disbanded factory that had been taken over by squatters in the 1980's. Squatters were people who just found an empty building and moved in. They didn't pay rent or anything, and over time squatters like Bethany got rental rights, and finally ended up owning entire floors of buildings. After years, a whole lot of poor starving artists ended up being real estate millionaires!"

Mum was on a roll, completely lost in her own mothball memories. Kids were squirming, the rain continued to pelt down, there was no way out. She hurtled on: "It was so much fun dreaming up theatre projects and putting them on in places like Theatre for the New City, or Interart, or Westside Arts. And if you got a good review in the New York Times, you'd get invited to amazing parties by amazing people, like when a great opera singer invited us for drinks at her place, or when the creator of the Living Theatre invited us over for a meal. But kids, the best story I remember was the opening night of that famous film about an emperor in China. You know the one, has anyone seen it?"

Everyone just looked blank or shook their heads. A day at school was more fun than being mummified by someone's mum on a rainy day. Mum looked puzzled and then made everyone promise to watch it. "Doesn't matter, it's a great movie. Anyway, the important thing is that the after party, you know, the party that comes after the official party, was at our loft!"

The fact was, none of the kids knew who she was talking about or why they were famous, and no one cared if a party was a party or an 'after party.' I looked across at Gilly. She reached into the lolly bowl and pulled out a row of teeth, then slipped them under her top lip and grinned at me. At least she was communicating with me; something was better than nothing. Then, just as I was thinking I might have a chance, Clancy reached into the bowl, got the last set of teeth and shoved them into his mouth. He tapped her on the shoulder to get her attention and they both cracked up. I imagined them as an old couple taking out their friggin' false teeth before bedtime and merrily cleaning them together over the bathroom sink. All the while Mum mindlessly barrelled on:

"That night the loft was packed with amazingly accomplished artists and a host of wannabes. I remember walking into my bedroom and seeing the director of the movie having a quiet chat with his entourage. Later in the evening, when I was formally introduced to him, I was so star struck, I went mute. My chin slumped onto my chest and stayed lodged there. All I could see were his shoes. They were brown leather. I kept praying to the universe to lift my chin up, to dislodge it, but on this particular occasion no angels were on duty, so my prayers went unanswered. I tried to speak but my mouth filled with saliva, then overflowed and dribbled down my chin, finally dropping unceremoniously onto the tip of the great director's shoe. Eventually the shoes moved away and I was able to lift my chin off my chest. I tried to see where he'd gone, but he had disappeared into the crowd."

Mum looked around expecting a barrel of laughter from the kids, but there was just an awkward silence and a few polite nods. Bryce had a little trail of red lolly dribble rolling down his chin. Aaron grinned at me, then slowly and deliberately let loose a blue stream of saliva out of the corner of his mouth and went cross eyed. I chucked a gummy bear at his head.

Mum was oblivious to the general boredom: "Later in the evening, I gathered up my courage and went over to the famous director and asked if there was anyone in the room that he would like to meet. He surveyed the sea of faces and pointed, 'Her, I would like to meet her, the one with the red hair.' It was my friend Suellen from Texas, another actress. She was busy batting her eyelashes at one of our Aussie friends who'd come over for a holiday. I walked over, tapped her on the shoulder and said, 'Suellen, I'd like you to meet Umberto.' Well, Suellen was oblivious and she resented the interruption to her fascinating conversation with a real live Aussie bloke. Not realising that this was no ordinary 'Umberto,' she heaved a sigh and in her Texan drawl said, 'Pleased to meet you Umberto and what do you do?' The famous director was taken aback. He smiled politely and humbly answered, 'I make films.' To which Suellen genuinely enquired, 'You mean home videos?' To which the director replied, 'No, I use film stock.'. Then Suellen gave the great director her sweetest smile and said, 'Well, that's nice Umberto.' Then she turned back to the Aussie bloke and said, 'Well now, what were you sayin' about them kangaroos?'"

Gilly giggled and it seemed genuine; not like she was just being polite. She caught my eye and I started to laugh. Her giggle was contagious. Before I knew it, we were just staring at each other laughing. I didn't even know what we were laughing at. I just remember thinking that maybe Mum's storytelling wasn't going to ruin my chances after all. It didn't take long for a few of the younger kids, high on sugar, to catch the contagion, and pretty soon a sort of mass hysteria engulfed the annex.

Mum stood up and called for order; even she didn't think the story was that funny, but the positive response spurred her on: "Well, by this time the famous director had had enough for one evening, so he gathered his entourage and headed for the door, but as luck would have it, a group of Aussies was just entering. They paused in the doorway and surveyed the crowd. Then one of them turned to the group of Italians and said, 'Gidday mate, where do we find the famous director? What's his name, Umberto?' One of the Italians stepped forward and said, 'I am Umberto.' Then another one stepped forward and said, 'No, I am Umberto' Then another stepped forward and declared the same identity, until finally the real Umberto stepped forward and declared, 'No, I am Umberto!' They played out the last scene of the film 'Spartacus'! You know when all the Spartans say that they're Spartacus, so the Roman soldiers can't arrest the real Spartacus."

None of the kids seemed to care about Spartacus, so Mum just kept going. "The Aussies stared at the film makers with no idea what was going on. Then one of them said, 'Yeah, right mate,' and pushed past into the room. The Italians got away and the Aussies spent the rest of the evening asking if anyone had seen Umberto!"

Mum had finished her story and gave herself a clap. I looked over at Gilly. She was actually clapping. Clancy gave her an affectionate nudge with his elbow and acted like he knew who Umberto was. Some of the younger kids were bored and yelled, "Tell us the one about the gun! Yeah, where did ya hide the gun?"

"Nah," said Mum. "I've just remembered another story. It might rain at Indented Head sometimes, but in New York City it snows!"

As the rain continued to pelt down and the cold

wind occasionally breached the cosy walls of canvas, I resigned myself to a very long afternoon, but as long as the girl with the silver hair was there, and as long as she wasn't too bored, I figured I could put up with Mum's rambling for a bit longer and so her next story began:

"The streets are narrow in Chinatown. In the dead of winter, the wind whistles and howls and turns snowflakes into razor blades. I huddled against Big El for protection. With his belt pulled tight around his waist, making his coat flare out like a skirt, and with a black woollen scarf draped over his head and knotted under his chin, he looked like an old Italian widow.

It was after midnight and we'd walked all the way from the theatre district, after our show, to get some Chinese food. Big El always said he knew Chinatown 'like the back of his hand', but on that particular night the back of his hand could have been a map of Istanbul for the amount of clarity it gave him. Even the cabbies avoided that part of town at that time of night.

We finally found a place that was open. There was nothing Big El liked more than a big hot bowl of duck soup around midnight, after a show. He wiped the grease from his mouth and grinned amiably. The Cantonese cook wandered over for a chat, but Big El couldn't speak Chinese and the cook couldn't speak English, so they settled on Italian. That was one of the things I liked about New York City; it was a place where there was always more than one way to skin a cat. The fluorescent lights of the restaurant gave everyone's face a kind of greenish glow. The place was full of weird types, and a person would have to be a bit weird to come out after midnight, in a blizzard, just for some Chinese food. It was full of alkies and junkies, slippin' and a slidin' in and out of consciousness, whores and their pimps, the odd millionaire and his mistress slumming it for the night, and amid all this experience, a note of innocence; a couple of young Asian students holding hands across the table and gazing into each other's eyes."

"Oh no, not a love story!" whinged Bryce. Hope put her hand over his mouth to shut him up. "I love, love stories!" she squealed. Mum put up her hand like a stop sign, "Don't worry Bryce, it's not a love story." She continued on:

"On another street a few blocks away, Mrs. Wong was closing her shop. She always closed up late. She often stayed downstairs in the shop 'til the early hours of the morning, dusting and polishing her precious objects, hundreds of rare oriental statues collected over many years, all antiques. She was worth a fortune but she wasn't afraid late at night because the Chinese Mafia always kept an eye out for the old people in the community. She dusted the jade horses and ivory warriors, then put them back on the shelves. She knew each one, where it had come from and who had brought it to her. Shelf upon shelf of ivory and jade figurines; they were her family. She liked the quiet. Her husband was long dead and her children were far away, finding their fortunes in countries she'd never been to. She hoped one day they would return. In the meantime, she polished and whispered to her tiny friends, occasionally singing in strange high-pitched tones, the old songs she'd learned as child, in that ancient land she had never returned to. It was a nightly ritual, never interrupted.

After we had finished our meal, Big El and I tried to find our way home. The snow lashed our faces and blurred our vision. The street lights were few and far between, and we were so far from our street, Houston Street, that it might as well have been in Texas. I was beginning to whine and the warm, cheery, 'just had a bowl of duck soup,' expression on Big El's face was beginning to fade. We made our way to the end of one street and turned a corner; nothing, just another row of shops lit by a street lamp. I glared at Big El. This definitely wasn't any street we recognized and there definitely weren't any cabs around. I wasn't pleased. There were times when Big El could be a pain. We had shared a lot of great adventures, but I wasn't enjoying this one. I was freezing, my face was numb, my feet were frozen solid and there was no movement in my fingers. I started to whimper, then I started to cry, then I gave up completely and began to howl, long and loud. I didn't want to die of frost bite in Chinatown at an early age. With his usual sense of compassion Big El told me to 'shut-up,' so I howled even louder.

Then Big El stormed off and I followed him. He kept walking faster and faster, and I tried to keep up, but in the heavy snowfall I lost sight of him. After a while it seemed like he had disappeared. I was terrified, I just kept moving in the general direction he was heading. Occasionally I'd catch a blurry glimpse of a figure up ahead. The sound of my own boots squishing into the snow became the footsteps of a stalker with murderous intent. I comforted myself with the thought that it was way too cold for evil types to be out combing the streets.

Eventually I came to a narrow alleyway, and there at the end, in the glow of a shop light, stood a bulky figure peering into a window. I walked towards it slowly. Yeah, it was Big El. I tapped him on the shoulder and he spun around, ready for a fight, but it was only me. He motioned for me to be quiet, and together we stood there watching a strange little old lady talking to a tiny ivory warrior.

Big El knocked on the door, but the old lady didn't hear. He banged louder and she looked up, fearful at first, but then she smiled when she realized it was just another old lady. She opened the door and Big El barged in, eager to get out of the cold. When he turned to face her, she froze, paralysed by fear. This wasn't another old woman, this was a man in a scarf, a man who had come to rob her! She breathed quickly, nervously, as Big El stumbled around the store admiring her wares, accidentally knocking things off shelves as he turned. He was a bull in a china shop.

I stood in the doorway watching the woman. She mustered all her courage and blurted out in her thick Chinese accent, 'Cosy inside!' Big El grinned and walked towards her, rubbing his hands together, delighted that they understood each other. 'Yes, yes, cosy inside!' The old lady's face registered absolute terror. She started pushing him out of the shop yelling 'Cosy inside! Cosy inside!' Big El looked at me, he didn't get it. So I grabbed him by the hand and dragged him outside. 'Not 'cosy' inside you idiot! It's closied inside!'

Yes, the streets are narrow in Chinatown. In the dead of winter, the wind whistles and howls and turns snowflakes to razor blades. We walked back up the alley, our teeth chattering as we snarled at each other, then from behind us we heard a thin voice calling 'Come back, come back!' We turned, and there was the old lady standing in her doorway, waving for us to come back. We hurried towards her, happy to be allowed to come inside, out of the cold. As we stood in the middle of the shop, not sure what to do with ourselves, she stared at us, then started to laugh. She pulled the scarf off Big El's head and laughed even louder; she bent double with laugher until tears ran down her wrinkly cheeks.

As we waited for the weather to ease, or for dawn to come, she showed us her statues and told us the stories of how she'd come by them. She gave us cups of tea and told us more stories; stories of sailors and shanty towns, opium dens and slavery, of wars and warlords. We sat and listened, grateful for the warmth, and even more grateful for her stories. Then slowly, slowly the wind died down, the snowfall became powder soft, and the first rays of dawn cast a pink glow through the window. It's a lot easier to find Houston Street in the light of day."

Bryce broke the spell, "I'm hungry. I want some Chinese food."

"I've only got toasties," said Mum, and she started slapping cheese slices on bread, and toasting them on the grill until they were all hot and yummy with the cheese dripping over the edges. As a dozen eager hands reached out for them, Clancy stood up and pulled Gilly to her feet, "Come on, let's go get some dinner at my place."

I waved lamely as they slipped through the flap of the annex, just as the rain started to ease and a little ray of sunshine pierced the sky.

Not another New York Story

After all the rain the day before, the next morning was bright and sunny. Mum was stretched out on her sun-lounge drinking her morning tea and staring out to sea. A pelican swooped along the shore, its wings spread wide, silhouetted against the morning sky. Another pelican flapped its mighty wings and rose to meet it, the comedy of their bills and bellies forgotten in the majesty of their flight. A tiny blue finch landed near Mum's feet, so she tossed it a few toast crumbs, then out of the blue she blurted; "I fired that famous actor."

"Who?" I asked.

"You know who, the guy from that T.V. series about the crime boss who loves his mum."

"Him! Why would anyone fire him?"

"He wasn't famous then, he was just doing his fifteen-minute Elvis monologue in some tiny downtown theatre. My friend Suellen from Texas dragged me along to see his show. He was great, just great, so I offered him a lead role in the play I was directing, a big two-hour play with just two characters. We didn't have any investors for the show, so everyone agreed to take a cut of the door, the ticket sales. Every morning we'd meet to start rehearsals but Jay would never have his lines down and there were a lot of lines to learn. I'd say, 'Hey Jay have you learned a few lines yet?' and he'd say in his Jersey drawl, 'Don't worry I'll get them down. I'm just feeling my way into the character.'

Three weeks into rehearsals, he still hadn't learnt any lines and I was big on learning lines. I used to say 'You can't really start acting until you've got your lines down.' It was a big play, so finally in desperation I said, 'Stuff it Jay, if you don't have ten pages of lines down by tomorrow, I'm gonna have to get someone else to play the role. We open in three weeks!' Then with absolute confidence he says, 'You're not gonna get rid of me,' and gave me one of his big bear grins. He was so bloody charming! The next day I asked if he had any lines down. 'Tomorrow, I'll get a few pages down by tomorrow,' he assured me. 'You're not gonna make it Jay. You're never gonna get all those lines down by opening night. It's not a fifteen-minute monologue, it's two hours of dialogue! Damn it, you're done! I'm gonna get a real actor!' I can still hear myself saying those dumb words, 'a real actor.' He said, 'Okay, then I'm gonna go to L.A.' And years later he got the lead role in that T.V. series. Every time I think about Jay, I feel like an idiot."

I asked Mum if she'd ever regretted not making it, not being famous, not being a 'real' actress. She insisted that you create your own life, that a person has to dream or imagine what they want, and then set about manifesting it, bringing it into reality. She was adamant that life doesn't just happen to you; you make it happen. It seemed to me she was just avoiding the question.

When I reminded her that she had dreamed of being an actress and didn't quite 'manifest it,' she got all worked up and said that she had dreamed of running her own theatre company and that's exactly what she did. She'd dreamed about getting rave reviews in the New York Times and that's exactly what happened. But when I complained that she wasn't famous, she insisted that fame robs you of your freedom. I argued that money, and power, and fame can get a person a lot of 'freedoms' that poverty and anonymity couldn't!

She said that one time when a telemovie she'd starred in had just come out and won a big award, and a play she was in was doing quite well, and a book she had written had just been published by a major publisher, which all amounted to a few people knowing who she was; she was trying on a dress in a department store, when a woman burst into the dressing room and asked for her autograph. Then on her way home on the tram, a man started talking to her as if he actually knew her. That night at a restaurant, the waitress forgot to take Mum's order because she was too busy prattling on about the telemovie she'd seen the night before. That was the day Mum decided that fame wasn't all it was cracked up to be.

Sometimes when she was telling her New York stories, I felt that she was not my mother, that she belonged to somebody else, and that the life she should be living was somewhere else and that the life she lived with me was just pretence, an adventure into the ordinary, some sort of research that she would put to good use at a later date.

When I was younger and told her that I thought she might not be my mother she agreed with me, and said that she was worried that I might not be her son; "Not one red curl on your head! Not even one blue eye! And a definite lack of wit! You missed the essential family gene! The foul German genes beat the Irish in the battle for your biome! You have your father to blame for that!"

Hope

Hope loved bugs: beetles, caterpillars, wasps, cockroaches, butterflies, Christmas beetles and spiders. She also loved crabs, sea urchins, lizards and birds, but most of all Hope loved dragon flies. She would water the Pigface plants that grew just outside her caravan, until dozens of dragon flies crept out from beneath the plant's waxy arms and bright pink flowers. She'd chase them holding out her bright pink cardboard box, then snap the lid down quickly once they were inside. She'd hold the box still, until she was sure that they were no longer frightened, then she'd gingerly lift the lid and watch them tap their heads with their spindly legs, until their heads spun a full three hundred and sixty degrees.

"Look! Look! Their heads are spinning!" she'd scream until my mother came running. She and Hope would stand dead still for ages, staring into the pink box, their two red heads knocking together. Red heads always seemed to be drawn to each other. If Hope and Mum weren't discussing bugs, they were moaning about freckles or sunburn or blisters. I guess Hope was the daughter my mother never had. Mum loved people with red hair. She said they were more joyful and honest than most. She said that I ought to marry a red head.

Gilly didn't have red hair. Her hair was soft and long and white, almost silver and it glistened in the sun like the scales of a fish.

The Big Bike Ride

I sometimes wondered if the mood of the people in camp affected the weather, or if the weather defined their mood. Why was it sunny so often at Indented Head when it was raining everywhere else? I thought of the American Indians doing rain dances. Maybe it was true, maybe it was possible with concerted collective effort, for humans to influence the weather. Maybe if enough people danced around a fire late at night and turned their attention to the skies, the drought in the Wimmera could be broken. I kept thinking that there was a whole lot more going on in the world than meets the eye, and maybe good old Shakespeare was right when he wrote: 'There are more things in heaven and earth, Horatio, than is dreamt of in your philosophy.'

Sometimes the mood in camp shifted and grey clouds rolled over as if called by some dark force. Squealing laughter subsided and kids slipped inside caravans to play games of Scrabble, or Monopoly, or Twister, as they listened to the rain beating down on their tin roofs. Families huddled together against the elements. The bad weather forced grown-ups and kids to be together. In our caravan, we sometimes read out loud to each other when we came to a good bit in a book. Mum's mandate: no play stations, no phones, no computers, no DVDs, just the mind stripped bare, to deal with itself. "Try thinking, it's enormously pleasurable," she'd say. I sometimes found it boring. There wasn't always a lot going on up there.

I peeked outside. The girl with the silver hair was standing on the shore, looking out to sea as usual. I don't know why I kept thinking of her as 'the girl with the silver hair' when I knew her name, but that's always who she was inside my head. She tilted her head up and opened her mouth to catch the rain on her tongue. I filled a tin cup with water and took it out to her.

"I brought you some water. You looked thirsty."

"Rain's precious where I come from."

"Where's that?"

"Wimmera, Saint Arnaud."

It sounded exotic, 'Saint Arnaud,' like some ski resort in France. I imagined snow-boarding with her down freshly powdered slopes.

"It's hot and dry. Sometimes it doesn't rain for years. It wears you down. It sucks you dry. You shrivel up before your time," she said.

"You don't look shrivelled to me," I muttered.

She looked at me as if I wasn't the sharpest pencil in the pack; as if I had a kangaroo loose in the back paddock.

"My father used to pray for rain."

"Used to?" I queried.

"He stopped. He just gave up."

"Gave up believing in God?"

"Just gave up believing in anything, or that things would get better."

"This too shall pass," I said.

"What?"

"Just something my mother says when things annoy her."

"My Dad always used to say, 'Out of the frying pan and into the fire.'" Gilly kept using the past tense when referring to her dad which was a bit weird. Then just as I was about to ask her about him, the rain eased a bit and a couple of kids burst out of one of the caravans and starting chucking their left-over fish 'n chips around, which attracted a flock of seagulls. They swooped and squawked and fought for chips, sending the kids into a squealing hysteria. I ducked as one gull swooped, barely missing my head. "I wonder where the pelicans are?" Gilly said, shifting the subject.

"Don't know. They disappear when it rains and they disappear at night, but they're always here at about 5 p.m. when people are gutting and filleting their fish. Have you seen them? They set up their ironing boards along the shore, like it's gonna be a mad laundry party, then they start wielding their knives, sharp as razors. The pelicans crowd around with their mouths wide open and the fishermen toss them fish heads and spines. You can stand right next to them, they're not afraid. The pelicans I mean, not the fishermen."

"Nothing is quite like a pelican." She smiled.

"Its beak can hold more than its belly can," I finished the rhyme as I looked at her. The rain had soaked her through and she shivered a little as she brushed a wet strand of hair out of her eyes. I thought she was going to leave, so I tried to keep the conversation going. "Yeah, when I was a little kid, I couldn't figure out why the boards were called ironing boards, when nobody did any ironing on them. My mother never ironed, so we didn't own one. I thought that maybe the fishermen used to bludgeon the fish with irons in the old-fashioned days to make sure they were dead, or that maybe some people ironed out the fillets to make them flat. Finally, I decided that maybe the boards used to be made out of iron instead of aluminium." From the way Gilly looked at me, I knew she was thinking; that there definitely was a kangaroo loose in the back paddock. So before she could escape, I tried my luck: "Do you want to go for a bike ride tomorrow? I know a place, Edwards Reserve, down passed St Leonards."

She looked at me as if she were looking right through me, "Zeke already asked me to go for a bike ride."

I thought, 'Zeke? Zeke doesn't even like bike-riding! He doesn't even bring a bike down here!'

"He said we could borrow your bike, and your mum's bike."

'Oh, nice one, Zeke!' I thought. "Yeah, that sounds great and I'll take my dad's bike, and we can all go together."

"What a nice surprise for Zeke," she said and smiled cheerfully. She seemed genuinely pleased that I was coming. Then the rain stopped just as a golden sheet of sunlight filtered through the clouds. It was funny how some people could change the weather with their smile.

That night as I tossed and turned on my camp bed, I thought that maybe Gilly would get on better with Zeke than me. At least his father prayed, and not just for himself but for everybody. At least that's what I thought ministers did, or maybe he just prayed for good surf. Either way, they both had fathers who prayed. My parents just believed that you make your own luck, you make your own bed and you lie in it, and that it's common sense to treat other people decently because then they'll treat you decently. As far as they were concerned the Ten Commandments were just a list of common-sense rules made by a tribe of people trying to get along in the desert, and any idiot with half a brain could have thought them up.

The next day we rode along the foreshore path, past mums and dads and grandparents stretched out on sun-lounges, reading or pretending to read, or just gazing out to sea, their minds a million miles away. I often wondered why people kept coming back decade after decade, but Indented Head was the kind of place from where you could go anywhere. I imagined sun-lounges floating across the ocean to Italy, or Brazil, or Egypt or Antarctica. People could go anywhere without moving a muscle. Or maybe they were just thinking about the past; who they could have been, what they could have done if they hadn't done what they did do, who they could have married, who they should have married, or maybe they contemplated dark secrets that once-a-year camping friends would never know about. Indented was a place where only the best was seen, and it seemed to bring out the best in people. There were so many people living so close together. They were polite to each other and if parents argued, they did it softly inside the caravan so as not to be heard by the people next door.

The oldies gazed out to sea, lost in far-away lands, lost in far-away love affairs, thinking about what they would do when they got back to work; some dreading the end of the holidays and others ready to get back to the real world. Only the kids seemed to be in the here and now, as they chased balls and snorkelled around the wreck.

Elvis was stretched out on his sun-lounge, his big tummy bursting through his lairy Hawaiian shirt, his new glass eye staring straight ahead, his good eye half shut, thinking or dreaming of who he might have been. He looked like Elvis, his voice was as sweet and smooth, and he knew all the Elvis songs. You could hear him playing his guitar and singing at night outside his caravan. When we were bored, we'd go and watch. Sometimes his wife would come out and join him. Mum said that she looked a bit like the country singer Dolly Parton, but she definitely didn't sound like her. Mrs. Elvis squawked like a cockatoo and sometimes when she started up, Harry mistook her for a galah and started shooting off blanks to shut up the squawking.

One night when Elvis was giving a particularly energetic rendition of 'Jail House Rock,' his glass eye popped out and rolled away. He offered a ten-dollar reward to anyone who could find it. We got our torches and searched high and low around his van but we had no luck. Days later we heard that Garry the golfer was whacking golf balls off the cliff towards the wreck, practicing his stroke, when someone handed him a golf ball that had an eye painted on it. He thought nothing of it at the time, but later he told Elvis that he thought his eye might be somewhere out near the wreck. We all went diving for it now and then, but no one ever found it. Elvis spent a whole summer with just one eye.

"Where ya going?" Clancy's voice broke my train of thought.

"Nowhere, just to Edwards Point," I answered.

"Bullshit, me and Aaron are coming too."

"Where ya going?" asked Bryce who followed Aaron around a lot.

"To the Reserve. You can't come," said Aaron.

"Yes I can, I'm getting Hope. We might get some bugs." Hope often followed Bryce around. They got their bikes and plastic containers for bugs.

"We're coming too!" I turned around and there was a flock of Zees flying after us, even the little twins Zelda and Zyana on their pink tricycles. Zeke turned around and yelled to his mum, who was stretched out on a towel on the sand, "Mum please!" She lifted her head drowsily, "Okay." Then she put two fingers in her mouth and whistled, a long sharp piercing whistle that would have burst the eardrums of any dog within five kilometres. Then she screeched, "Anyone under nine get back here!" We dropped a few Zees in an instant.

We were just about level with the boat shed when

the Westies sprang out from behind the bushes and blocked our path: Nelson, Shelton, Gus, Brad, Zeth, Zed and a bunch of girls in bikinis. The Westies always had girls hanging around. I noticed that Clancy's little sister Miranda was with them, except she didn't look that little anymore. She was only about a year younger than me and Clancy, but we never took any notice of her when we were growing up, mostly because she was a girl and did girl stuff, and always seemed to have her own group of friends. But on New Year's Eve she always fought with us. She caught me staring at her and poked her tongue out. Very mature I thought, and gave her a cross-eyed look. She cracked up. I had to admit she had nice teeth.

"No one passes until you give us ten bucks," Zeth taunted his big brother.

"Shit," I muttered.

"Cut the crap. New Year's Eve is over," shouted Clancy. Those guys were trolls.

"We didn't bring any money, we're just going for a bike ride," growled Zeke, "Piss off."

I was beginning to understand how Odysseus had felt back in ancient Greece: You just get over one problem and another one pops up, but the Westies were hardly sirens.

"Where ya going?" demanded Gus.

"To the Reserve."

"We're coming too," said Shelton. "C'mon guys, get the bikes."

"Can we come too?" asked one of the girls.

"Course you can, get your bikes," said Nelson.

I wondered why those guys always had girls around, but I guess if I was honest, it wasn't hard to figure out. Brad was always cracking jokes and making people laugh, Gus could play the guitar and sing. Zeth and Zed were only about fifteen at the time, but they looked at least seventeen. They had big kind hearts and were willing to help anyone with anything, whether it was setting up a camp site or chasing some kid's floaty blowing out to sea. They were always taking the girls for a sail in their two-man dinghy, and when they got a bit older, they saved up for a jet ski, and contrary to my mother's theory, girl's love going for rides on the back of jet skis! Nelson was quiet and sensitive, but unbelievably good looking, and Shelton was a real Ranga, a red head with Viking blood. He had the word 'good,' written all over his face. He was a genuinely decent human being.

And what was I? Half-way between one nothing and another nothing, no distinguishing features, mental or physical. Once when I told my mother I was a nothing, she smiled sweetly and said, "Of course you're nothing darling! You're a writer! All writers sublimate their own ego in order to plumb the depths of others." Sometimes she really made me want to puke.

I looked behind me. Everyone was there, a regular family outing. Even Jack had gotten wind of it and had ditched his diving gear for a romantic romp. I looked at Gilly. She just grinned and shrugged, and kept on riding.

We rode fast along the beach path until we reached the big hill at St Leonards, where a shady row of giant Cyprus trees cooled us down as we whizzed past. We continued on until we reached the steep path leading down to St Leonards yacht club. Most of the boys took the drop at breakneck speed and whipped around the bend at the bottom, skidding with professional precision. We rode past the big houses built so close to the shoreline, that from the inside they must have felt like giant ships floating on a private apple-green sea; some day to be swept away under the impartial gaze of climate change.

Finally, we reached the start of Edwards Reserve and got off our bikes, sweat running down our faces. Me and Zeke took swigs of water from the bottles attached to our bikes. Everyone else stared at us.

"Shit, didn't any of ya bring any water?" demanded Zeke.

No one said anything. Then Zeb piped up, "Give us some of yours. Go on, Mum said ya gotta share!"

"That was lollies, not water!" snapped Zeke and handed his little brother the flask of water.

"Just one gulp each," I said and handed mine to Gilly who took a gulp and passed it on.

The place was still, incredibly still and hot, like a thick blanket of heat had been thrown over it. The sea breeze didn't reach all the way into the Reserve. There were strange buzzing noises that didn't let up, like all the insects on the planet were having a confest, and then there was the insane chirping of crickets, coming from deep within the scrub. I thought crickets only started up at night.

"Crickets!" squealed Hope, as a dragon fly whizzed past her head.

"I don't want to go in. This place is creepy!" whinged one of the Zees.

"Then go home," snapped Zeke.

"Not by myself," said the younger Zee.

"Then you'll have to come with us."

"It's got snakes!" cried one of the bikini girls, pointing to a sign with a big swirly snake painted on it.

Hope was busy reading all the details: "There are big browns; highly poisonous. It says to seek medical attention if you get bitten."

"Brilliant! Brilliant advice. Good to know the Bayside Authority is on the job," I said sarcastically.

When everyone had had a gulp of water, Zeke and I snapped the empty bottles onto our bikes and took off. "Shit, why did you have to invite so many people?" I trolled Zeke.

"Shut up dickhead, it was supposed to be just me and Gilly. I don't even know how you got to be here," he snarled as we rode in single file along the narrow path through kilometres of low-lying scrub and over the rickety, winding slats of the wooden walkway that passed over the salt marshes. I stared out across the spinifex; it looked like some place in Africa. I half expected a lion to leap out of the scrub. I remembered hearing that there was supposed to be quick-sand out there somewhere.

"Me and Bryce are stopping here to get some bugs," called out Hope.

"Okay, we'll pick you up on the way back," yelled Aaron.

The wooden slats ended at the start of a narrow track, not much wider than a bike wheel. It ran through kilometres of sword grass that sliced our ankles as we whizzed by. The eerie silence was occasionally punctured by a choice expletive as the riders engaged with their pain.

"I'd rather be bitten by a friggin' snake than ride through this friggin' grass," cried one of the girls.

"Careful what you wish for!" Clancy yelled back.

A snake slithered from one side of the track to the other, right in front of my wheel. I swerved to miss it and braked. Clancy crashed right into the back of me and we tumbled into a big Spinifex bush.

"Shit! Ya retard, what are ya doing?" growled Clancy.

"Avoiding a snake," I whispered. "Don't let the others know, I don't want them freaking out."

"You okay?" asked Gilly as she rode past.

"Having a bit of a cuddle fellas?" quipped Aaron as he whizzed past.

By the time me and Clancy had untangled ourselves and our bikes, we were on the end of the line.

As we rode on through the golden six o'clock light, I heard one of the younger kids up ahead whinging about being hungry; "Why did we leave so late? It's almost dinner time?"

"It wouldn't have taken so long if you lot weren't all tagging along," I yelled, gripping the handlebars and trying to ignore the ache in my legs.

"Why didn't you tell me you were going?" demanded Clancy.

"I didn't need any more competition."

"It's obvious she likes me and Zeke. You don't stand a chance."

"She just talks to you because she feels sorry for ya."

"Bullshit, I make her laugh."

Clancy and I bantered on, getting more and more on each other's nerves. Finally we got to The Spit, the place where Zeke and Gilly and I had planned to watch the sunset. The place was special; we had discovered it one year when we were kids and had nicked off without permission. I remember sitting there in silence with Clancy and Aaron and Zeke, watching the most spectacular, glowing, pulsating sunset we'd ever seen. It was like a magical scene from heaven, or Mt Olympus, created to herald the arrival of gods or angels. It was a spectacular opening to another universe, a place where only goodness existed. Every summer since then, the four of us have made the pilgrimage to The Spit, to experience the sheer bliss of transcendent beauty.

Everyone dumped their bikes and walked over the sand towards the lookout point. When we got there, we saw it had been taken over by a bunch of older guys, maybe in their late twenties. They looked like they had been there for a while; beer cans were chucked all over the sand and there were a couple of empty whiskey bottles lying around. We could smell weed, as one of the guys passed a joint to his mate. All-in-all it wasn't a good sign, but for some dumb reason we just kept walking towards the look-out point, trusting in the infinite goodness of human nature.

As we tried to pass the group of men, Zeb whinged that he was thirsty. One of the drunk guys handed him a can of beer, "Take this mate, that'll quench it." Zeb took the can but Zeke wrenched it out of his hand, tore off the ring and took a long gulp himself, then he poured the rest onto the sand, glaring at the drunk guy.

"Don't waste me brew kiddies," the guy slurred and kicked Zeke in the shin.

"Let's go home," whined Zadie who should have been back at camp, "I'm hungry."

"Hey girly, I got some lollies. Ya want some?" One of the dickheads staggered over to Zadie and put a couple of white pills in her hand, "Ya won't feel hungry if you swallow them," he snickered. I leapt at Zadie, snatched the pills out of her hand and trampled them into the sand.

"You lot don't seem to value our generosity," snarled one of the other dickheads, who kept throwing a spear from a speargun at his mate's feet. The guy was jumping and twisting out of its way, then squealing like a pig when the spear came too close. Then quick as a flash, the nut-case turned and threw the spear at Zeke's feet. Zeke pulled the spear out of the sand, paused for effect, then in full athlete mode sent it soaring way over their heads and out to sea.

"You fuckin' little bastard," yelled the nut-case and leapt at Zeke. Then one of the younger kids kicked sand into the face of one of the other men. All hell broke loose. Kids were running and screaming in all directions, chased by druggies and drunks. Kids tossed handfuls of rotting seaweed in the bastards' faces. The shitheads roared in retaliation, as kids twisted and turned to escape their angry, grasping hands. One arsehole held Zeth tight around the neck with a thick tattooed arm. Zed whacked the guy so hard across the face with a long leathery wad of seaweed, it left a welt so red it would take weeks to fade. Suddenly a Border Collie appeared out of nowhere and started barking wildly, and running in circles in an attempt to round everyone up. The shrill squawk of seagulls sent out an alarm, as the stench of rotting seaweed drifted over the chaos. I remember the sky was a vast expanse of pink, mauve and orange. And right above us floated a great golden billowing cloud in the shape of an angel, with enormous silver-tipped wings; her golden gown trailing behind her like Haley's Comet.

Then through the mayhem we heard a piercing scream that made the hairs on the back of my neck stand up. We all looked over and saw that one of the shitheads had pushed Gilly over and pinned her to the ground. He was slobbering all over her and grinding his groin against her. Zeke, Clancy and I caught each other's eyes and together we ran over and dragged him off. As I helped Gilly to her feet, Clancy yanked the dickhead's pants down to his ankles. He stumbled backwards and collapsed in the sand. Clancy towered over him. Then, conjuring up the spirit of the great Dundee, Clancy glared a down at the man's dick and bellowed, "I don't know what you call that nonentity between ya legs!" Then Clancy whipped his own shorts down to half-mast and roared, "But this is a penis!" The dickhead stared in horror and tried to slither away. I don't know if he was more intimidated by Clancy's appendage or his use of formal language: 'nonentity,' 'penis.' I'd certainly never heard Clancy refer to a dick as a 'penis' before. We all roared with laughter. Most of the guys had caught a glimpse of Clancy's package at some time or another, because when they were younger, Clancy and Jack were always mooning people when they least expected it.

Then one of the drunks went hysterical and started prancing around laughing and screaming, "This is a penis!" His moron mates didn't find it quite so funny. Then Jack, fearing for his brother's life, mooned them all, leapt on his bike and rode off. The Border Collie and a couple of the morons chased him. Brad, Gus and Shelton grabbed their bikes and were fast on their heels. The shithead lying in the sand struggled to his feet and made a grab for Clancy, but he got caught up his undies again and face planted into the sand. Clancy pulled up his own shorts, leapt onto the guy's back, yanked his head back, then planted his face back in the sand. The arsehole writhed as Clancy held him down. A couple of mean looking bastards were eyeing off the girls. "Nelson, get them back to camp!" I yelled.

"Zeb, Zadie, get back to camp! Zara, take them home! Zeth, Zed get the fuck out of here!" screamed Zeke. They all ran for the bikes and took off. Then one of the shitheads dashed over, grabbed a bike and was chasing the kids. Zeke picked up another one of the spears lying in the sand and let it fly, landing it right in the spokes of the back wheel. The bike crashed to the ground and the arsehole tumbled into a clump of sword grass.

By that stage there was only Clancy, Aaron, Zeke and me, left behind to face four mad bastards. I looked around for Jack, but he hadn't come back. He should have come back by then. The two dickheads chasing him hadn't come back either. I reminded myself that these morons might be off their nuts, but they probably didn't want to face murder charges, and Jack rabbit was wily as a fox. I stared up at the sky to make sure the angel was still watching over us, but somehow her wings had floated away and her gown was merely a capitulating comet on a downhill descent of dust particles.

"What're ya doing? Composing ya next poem? We're looking death in the eye and you're staring at the friggin' sky! Wake up ya moron!" Clancy jolted me out of my musings as he elbowed me in the ribs.

"You calling me a moron kid?" croaked one of the shitheads.

"Nah, I was just talking to me mate. He's not all there," said Clancy tapping the side of his head.

"Yeah, sometimes he has these fits, jerks around and froths at the mouth. It happens when he's upset," added Aaron.

I took my queue. I sometimes thought that if I didn't make it as a writer, I could become an actor. So I started to tremble and then I started to shake. I rolled my head and began to dribble. I stared one of the bastards in the eye and made myself go cross eyed. Then I let out a howl, like a crazed galah, spun around, and collapsed in the sand. I lay there jerking around, my eyes pinned at a point in the pink sky. I coughed up a great ball of green slime and let it roll out of my mouth and down the side of my chin. Then in a moment of inspiration, I went completely still, my eyes fixed on a pale pink cloud floating blithely in the fading sunset.

"You've killed him. Ya fuckin' morons! Ya going to go

to jail for the rest of ya lives!" screamed Zeke.

"Bullshit, he's just unconscious," muttered one of the shitheads.

"He may not be dead yet, but he will be if we don't get him to a hospital!" yelled Aaron.

"The police are gonna get you bastards. You've killed me best mate," Clancy accused them.

Then Clancy fell to his knees and lay his head on my chest, sobbing and howling like a bereaved widow. It was as if he was going for an Academy Award. I felt like cuffing him one in the ear, but I kept still. Then Aaron started up in a harsh whisper, cold as ice; "I've seen the eyes of fish when they're dying. At first, they stare back at you as if they can see right through you, as if they know who you are, as if they know all you've done wrong and all you're ever gonna to do wrong. Their eyes fill with love for you, 'cos you're only human, then slowly a creamy film passes over their pupils and their eyes go white, they don't see anymore." Then Aaron stared down into my eyes and hissed "Shshshsh they've started to turn creamy." At that moment, I knew there was more to Aaron than meets the eye. Given the competition, I was tempted to leap up and do my best rendition of Hamlet's, 'To be or not be,' speech but I kept still.

Then out of the blue, one of the dickheads said, "Hey mate, I've got a car. Maybe we should get him to Geelong hospital."

"Nah, me mum told me never to get into cars with strangers," quipped Aaron. Then he pulled my eyelids right back and took a closer look, "There's still blood around the rims, he might pull through if we can get him conscious." Then he started slapping my cheeks.

"Yeah, maybe if we get him standing the blood might pump to his head." Clancy wiped his phoney tears away and hauled me to my feet. "Feeling better, mate?" he asked.

I staggered forward and shook my head as if to try and clear it. "Groggy, a bit groggy. Water, I need water," I croaked.

The arsehole who had pinned Gilly to the ground pulled a beer out of his Eski. "Here mate, get this into ya" and he opened the can for me. I took great gulps.

"Thanks mate." Why was I calling him mate? The guy was a bastard. If we hadn't hauled him off Gilly, things could have turned out a lot worse.

"Let's go before it gets too dark," said Zeke.

"Yeah, take it easy guys," said one of the arseholes.

We walked back to where we'd left our bikes in the sand. I looked back at our tormentors lighting a nice little camp fire right at the end of the lookout point. They had a perfect view, all the way across Swan Bay.

We rode in silence along the narrow track, the tufts of spear grass slashing at our shins, their blonde mohawks reflecting slivers of moonlight, creating a silvery gauntlet to guide our way out. When we got to the wooden bridge leading over the salt marsh, Aaron braked hard and we slammed on our brakes behind him.

"What're ya doing? Ya friggin' idiot," complained Clancy.

"Bryce! Bryce and Hope, we left them here, remember, to get their friggin' bugs."

"They probably went back with the others," said Zeke.

"Not necessarily, everyone was in a panic. Maybe they didn't stop and look for them," I said.

We started calling out, "Bryce! Hope! Hope! Bryce!" The silence was deafening.

The moon had risen a little more and cast an eerie silver glow over the salt marsh. Weird shapes and shadows seemed to dance over the surface. "I'm not going out there," I whispered.

"They would've gone home when it started to get dark. Hope's a smart kid," Clancy whispered.

"Why are we whispering?" whispered Zeke.

"Hope might have found her way back, but Bryce wouldn't have gone back, he would've come looking for me," said Aaron.

"If he was looking for you, he would've followed the track to The Spit and we would've bumped into him. They must have gone back," I said.

"It's pointless staying here. Let's just get back and find out if they're there. If they're not, we'll come back and look for them," said Clancy as pragmatic as ever.

"Yeah, with torches and a few mates to back us up," said Zeke.

We rode back along the track, past St Leonards, under the gloomy cedars, all the way to the Indented Head boat shed, where Jack and the Westies were waiting for us.

"Where the hell have you lot been?" yelled Jack, and hauled Clancy off his bike, wrestling him to the ground. "We were worried sick! We were just about to come looking for ya."

"Have you seen Bryce and Hope?" asked Aaron.

"Yeah, they're over at Hope's caravan categorising their bugs. They got a whole container full. Shelton and Gus spotted them on the other side of the salt marsh, after we ditched those fuckwits who were following me. We walked them back to their bikes and rode home with them. God, Hope's a pain! She never shuts up. She jabbered all the way back about weird bugs and barmy birds flying all the way from Siberia to mate at Edwards Reserve, and dogs eating the birds while they mated in the Chassey Saw Sedge. What the hell is Chassey Saw Sedge?"

"Grass," I answered. "It said so on one of those info boards."

"Who the hell reads info boards?" demanded Jack. "And Bryce kept saying that he was gonna go find Aaron, but I said I'd whack him in the ear if he didn't get on his bike and ride home."

"What about those dickheads that were chasing you?" asked Clancy.

"You mean these dickheads?" and Jack waved at the Westies.

"No, the other dickheads, you dickhead."

"Ditched them pretty quick. They weren't much of a match for Jack Rabbit. Besides me mates were bringing up the rear weren't you fellas?"

Gus and Brad and Shelton grinned.

"We left them wandering around the salt marsh with that dog snarling and running circles round them. I don't think he liked them any better than we did!"

I looked at Nelson. "Girls, okay?"

"Yeah, they're fine." He caught my eye. "Gilly's fine."

Ads

The family that usually camped next door left early one year, and new people pulled onto the site for the final week of the holidays. Mum was putting the cover on the gazebo. Every morning, she'd toss the cover over the central pole and then drag it over the frame. It took her forever and she refused any help. She said it was like getting a basketball into a hoop, and kept her on her toes. The new neighbour, a big man with a protruding beer belly, ambled over and tried to pull the cover out of Mum's grasp, insisting on giving her a hand. Mum tugged the cover out of his clutches and insisted that she didn't need any help. A tug of war developed, until Mum finally pulled so hard, the man lost his balance and tumbled into a prickly shrub at the front of our site.

Then his wife, a slender woman with a twinkle in her eye, wandered over, handed Mum a broom and said, "Here try this, just lever the cover up on the broom. You don't need a man if you've got a broom." Mum paused to think. This was technical stuff. Then she hugged the woman and declared it was pure genius. Mum has been hoisting the gazebo cover with a broom ever since.

As much as Mum liked the woman, she simply didn't see eye to eye with the husband. He'd get up bright and early each morning and switch on his radio full blast, because he must have been a bit deaf. He'd leave it on all day with the cricket or the horse races blasting away, punctuated with plenty of ads. Now what Mum liked most about Indented Head were the sounds of nature, the wind, the waves, and the sound of kids laughing. Perhaps she could have put up with the bloke's radio if he'd been listening to a bit of jazz or classical, but there were four things Mum hated listening to and they were; cricket, football, horse racing, and ads! After two days of it, her patience ran out. She ambled over and in her best ocker drawl said, "G'day mate."

"G'day," the man answered cheerily, eager for a chat.

"Luv ya radio station, mate. D'ya mind givin' me the number on the dial, so's I can tune mine into it, that way we'll be in sync."

"Sure," said the man, thinking that he might have misjudged my mother and that she might have been that rare breed of female that enjoyed listening to choice programs like the cricket and the horse races.

"Yeah mate, the best bits are the ads mate, and if ya don't have 'em up good and loud, ya might miss 'em, and if ya missed 'em, ya wouldn't know what to buy, and if ya didn't know what to buy, where'd ya be mate? Nowhere! 'Cos that's what life's about mate; ya listen to the ads and then ya go out and buy what they tell ya to buy! So, I reckon if I put my radio on the same station as yous, and we both turn 'em up good and loud, then everyone will know what they oughta be buyin'. Ya gotta share ya knowledge mate!"

Mum put her hands on her hips and stared him down. He cocked his head to one side and squinted at Mum, then scratched his chin. He tried to get a grip on her meaning; maybe she was pulling his leg, or maybe she was right, maybe people did need to know what to buy. Either way he had the distinct feeling she was stark raving bonkers and the quickest way to get rid of her was to hand over the number on the dial. Mum thanked him and went inside, where she set the radio on the same station as the neighbour, then turned it up as loud as she could, opened the window facing the man's van and let it blast all day, while she read peacefully under the cedars down near the jetty.

At dinner time the man came over and asked Mum if she wouldn't mind turning down the radio. She smiled amiably and said, "Nah mate, I wouldn't want ya to miss any ads."

The man just stared at her. He still didn't know if she was pulling his leg, or if she was a bit retarded. The funny thing was, the couple didn't come back the following year.

Treason

I was walking past Harry's caravan one day when I heard the sound of sobbing, big guttural sobs. We'd all heard strange sounds coming from Harry's van at different times; screaming, pots banging and snatches of dialogue, as he wrestled with ghosts from his war years, but I'd never heard him cry. I lifted the flap of his annex and crept inside. "Are you okay, Harry?"

I climbed up the step into his van. I loved Harry's van. From the outside it was just another old rust bucket like ours, but on the inside it was magic; a kind of tribute to both war and peace, and except for the greasy gas stove that needed a good scrub, the place was pretty tidy. There were Vietnam war photos stuck to the cupboards, like the famous one of a naked kid screaming and running down a road with his arms spread out like a fragile bird, while bomb blasts blanket the background. Right next to it was a poster of a big PEACE sign, and next to that an old record cover of a musician with afro hair and a headband, and the words 'War, What Is It Good For?' printed underneath. On top of the cupboards were jars full of old war medals he'd collected from op-shops over the years, and on a narrow window ledge above the table was a parade of toy soldiers and tanks.

Harry was slumped on the end of his bed, holding some sort of letter. "Look what they sent me. After all my years of loyalty! I mean, I got used to the army treating us veterans like shit; no one believin' us when we said we weren't well, then givin' us a quick physical and sending us on our way with a 'You'll be right mate.' And I *was* alright, I was alright because I found me little piece of paradise, here, right here!"

Harry was one of a few oldies who had a kind of permanent lease; some sort of outdated arrangement with the park authorities which meant they could camp all year.

"But this!" Harry waved his letter in the air, tears streaming down his face. "This is treason! I'll kill the bloody bastard!"

"What bastard Harry? Who are you talking about?" I asked.

"The bloody ranger! He brung this bullshit this morning. They want me to leave! They say I'm a disturbance, that I'm frightening the kids! Did you ever see me frighten a kid? Did ya?"

I stared at the worn-out lino on the floor of the van. I

got lost in the mottled green and brown pattern which reminded me of camouflage gear. I saw Harry crawling on his belly shooting kids. "Nah, you never frightened us," I lied.

Harry waved the letter in the air again. "I've been here over forty years! It's not fair, this doesn't make sense!".

It was true, it didn't make any sense, but the camp ranger often did things that didn't make sense. I remembered the time when he stuck a notice on the front of everyone's caravan and in the toilet blocks, that said, 'Campers must adhere to common sense at all times.' After a couple of days and after a few particularly absurd arguments with Dad, Mum tore down the notice, marched up to the office with it, and announced that her husband had not been 'adhering to common sense at all times.' She demanded that the ranger knock some common sense into Dad. The next thing we knew, all the other mums were marching up to the office with their notices, demanding that the ranger do something about their husband's lack of common sense. A few days later the ranger removed all the notices from the toilets and the laundry block.

"I'm not leavin'!" cried Harry. "I'll kill every last one of them rangers!" Harry started loading his rifle with rubber bullets. "I'll kill one first, and when they send in the next fella, I'll shoot him too. I'll pop 'em off one by one!" The wrinkles on his face deepened as he scowled in absolute rage and aimed his gun at me. I didn't know who he was seeing when he looked at me, so I stood stock still and tried to stay calm.

"They won't send them in 'one by one,' Harry. They'll

send in the CAT team, and they will take you away and lock you up. You've got to calm down. We'll think of something."

When I told Mum what had happened to Harry, she got a petition together to say that Harry was perfectly sane. All the kid's signed willingly, but some of the grown-ups demanded a proper psychiatric assessment.

In the end Harry wasn't allowed to stay. They took him away and put him in some home for veterans. It was so far from the sea, he never heard a seagull squawk again.

Divorce

Down at Indented Head they say; 'the family that camps together stays together,' but I had a funny feeling this adage didn't hold true for my family. Dad had stopped coming down for the whole season. He would set up camp, then clear off after a week. He'd say that he was sick of everything being so predictable; the people were the same, the scenery was the same, the wreck was the same, the pelicans were the same. Then I'd always say:

'There's no bird like the Pelican,
Its beak can hold more than its belly can.'

The first seven years or so, he'd always say that he loved the place because no day was ever the same and the sea always shifted currents and colours. It was a changing panorama of pale, lime green seas with distant strips of olive that occasionally turned aqua, then deadly shades of grey on dull days. For him the great arc of the sky was never the same. He'd sit there gazing at the fluffy white shapes drifting over the blue background, or he'd point to great gun metal grey cumulus clouds, gathering in the west bringing storms. He used to appreciate it all and he had painted it dozens of times.

He would paint it and Mum would sit next to him writing about it. They seemed content, drifting through the summers in each other's company. In many ways they were a lot alike, both artists, both temperamental, and both pretty insensitive and intolerant of other people, which I figured was because they'd both been beautiful when they were young. Beautiful people seemed to get away with a few personality flaws that more ordinary types had to face up to. There was something similar in their facial structure; they both had high cheekbones, which seemed to be an hereditary endowment that obviously skipped a generation, I noted when I observed my own flat features in the mirror.

Whereas Dad grew more resentful of the daily routine down at Indented Head, Mum revelled in it. She had a high tolerance of repetition. She said it came from doing theatre for decades. She'd say, "Sometimes we'd do the same show six or seven times a week; same words, same gestures, same emotional intent, night after night. The pleasure lay in finessing the moment, perfecting the detail."

She brought the same attitude to Indented Head; 'finessing' the detail of her observations or perceptions. She'd argue that the place was never boring because the kids were always growing and changing, and that they were all so different, and the differences became more pronounced each year. She said that each kid was like an amazing character from a novel, "Look at Jesse and Clancy, they used to be so much alike, but now Clancy has become louder and funnier and more extroverted while Jesse has receded inside his shell and become shyer and more introverted." When she said stuff like that, it felt like I had drawn the short straw, and somehow my personality was set in stone, and I was doomed to be an introverted lonely bore for the rest of my life.

The night Dad left, I stood outside the annex of the caravan listening to them argue. I guess most of the people camped nearby were listening as well.

"It's not all the same! The kids change, the light changes!' yelled Mum.

"I'm not interested in other people's kids!" yelled Dad.

"That's obvious! You're only interested in yourself!"

"I'm an artist! I'm interested in light! Light and shade!"

"Put out the light and then put out the light," snapped Mum, quoting a bit of Shakespeare. I guess she was referring to the death of Desdemona, in Othello.

"Don't you telling me about light! I'm an artist!" shouted Dad.

"Stop speaking in pigeon English, it's irritating. It's, 'don't you TELL me about light," screeched Mum.

"That's vot I said!" bellowed Dad.

"It's not what you said! You said 'telling' with ING," cried Mum, totally frustrated at the bastardisation of the English language.

"Vot? Vot, are you talking?" queried Dad, unable to fathom what she was talking about.

"You see, you just did it again! Talking 'about!' You forgot the 'about!'"

"Vot are you talking about!"

"You! You don't speak English properly!" spluttered Mum.

"Ve've been living together for seventeen years and suddenly you don't like the vay I talk! It's ridiculous!"

"We've been coming here for sixteen years and suddenly you don't like it here!"

"I stopped liking it here five years ago," retorted Dad.

"I stopped liking you five years ago!" screeched Mum.

My parents were getting louder and louder. It was embarrassing. People were popping their heads out of caravans to hear better. Clancy and Aaron turned up and huddled next to me. Clancy started mimicking my mother, so I elbowed him in the gut.

Aaron whispered, "Maybe they're gonna get divorced."

"They can't get divorced, 'cos they've never been married. They've just lived together for years which makes me a bastard."

"Yeah, I always thought that," whispered Aaron in an attempt to cheer me up.

"Shut up!" hissed Clancy and inched the annex flap open slightly so he could hear better.

We waited in silence for the next round. We waited and waited. The silence was deafening. The whole caravan park held its breath.

My parents used to say that they were free-spirits and that marriage was just a conspiracy set up by the church and state to grab more taxes. I never could figure out how that worked. When I was little, I used to beg my parents to let me see their wedding photos, because all my friends' parents had wedding photos hung on their walls, or propped up on shelves. Finally, Mum pulled out a photo of her and Dad in full blown Louis XIV costumes. They both wore big white fluffy wigs, and Mum's dress was enormous. She looked beautiful and genuinely happy. Dad held her hand outstretched. That photo made me really happy. They both looked so regal, I just assumed it was their wedding photo and that I was part of a royal blood line. I used to think that one day they would reveal my true identity to me, but as I stood outside the annex listening to my parents fight, all I could think of was the guillotine.

"That's it, I go!" yelled Dad. The whole caravan park let out its breath.

"It's 'I'm going.' Speak English!" corrected Mum.

"But you are not going, you are staying," screamed Dad.

"Yes, I'm staying," whispered Mum.

At that moment Dad pushed open the flap of the annex and nearly bowled us over as he stormed out. He only paused for a moment to look at me, ignoring my friends. "I go now. Look after your mum." Then he was gone, disappearing among the caravans in the fading light.

I wondered where he would go; I thought of all the places he had travelled to in his younger days. I wondered if he might hit the old hippie trail again and take me with him. In that moment as I watched him storm off, I realized I knew more about where he'd been, than who he was.

A few months later Dad rented himself a house in Ballarat, which was a bit strange for a person wanting to escape Indented Head, given that most of the people who camped there actually lived in Ballarat.

Once, when I went up to visit him, he said, "Ballarat is a strange place. Ven I valk down the street, I get the feeling I've seen all the faces before."

"You have Dad, you have," I said.

Fish

The cold early morning swim out to the wreck didn't do much to dull the thud in my head. Clancy by contrast was immune to the after effects of alcohol. It had been a long night after Dad left, and instead of comforting Mum, I'd snuck off with Aaron and Clancy. We'd looted the alcohol from the special Eski Aaron's dad kept in their annex, and smuggled it down to the beach.

We chewed over parental relationships for a while, until we got bored with the topic and tried to think of excuses Aaron could give to his dad when he discovered the missing beers. Clancy thought he could blame the theft on a few thirsty pelicans, or rogue locals who had been known to raid the camp occasionally. Finally, Aaron decided the best bet was to go back, own up to the truth and say he was commiserating with a mate who'd had some bad news. Everyone would know about it in the morning anyway. Clancy and I decided to stay up and watch the sunrise.

It started as a hazy golden globe floating on the horizon, before defying gravity and inching its way skyward, daring us to hold its piercing gaze.

As we lounged on the wreck looking down through the crystal-clear water at a school of fish, all I wanted was silence, but Clancy was definitely feeling chirpy.

"You know what I like about fish?" I didn't bother to respond. "They travel in schools, big schools making big shapes in the water."

"Yeah, like flocks of birds making shapes in the sky. As above, so below." I struck a philosophic note, hoping to put an end to the conversation.

"What?"

"Nothin'."

"Fish need each other. A fish alone is just a shark snack," he continued on.

"Bullshit, a school of fish draws attention. A shark can power through it and take out half the school, or at least three or four classes, whereas a solo fish can hide in a patch of seagrass and never be noticed. It can survive."

"No man is an Island," quoted Clancy.

"Oh, deep Clancy, very deep! But we're not talking about men, we're talking about fish!"

"Same thing, it's all about survival," Clancy concluded.

"Yeah, but you know what they say," I was warming to the challenge, "Man can't live on bread alone."

"Right, a man needs meat."

"Bullshit, it means people need stories to survive."

"What kinda stories?"

"I don't know; stuff like overcoming adversity, courage, friendship. I don't know just stuff; footsteps to follow in."

"Men just need meat and sex, that's all we're talking about, and the fact is you don't eat enough meat 'cos ya dad's a vego, and ya probably won't ever have sex 'cos you're so friggin' ordinary."

I pondered Clancy's incisive observations and concluded that there was no point in opposing what was basically true, so I decided to run with the theme: "That's true, females are attracted to good looking guys and not just good looking, they like bad boys. I read about it; there's these really good-looking prisoners, like murderers and rapists, who get thousands of love letters from women all over the world. Why? 'Cos they've got deep set eyes and overhanging brows. They look like wolves. They can hunt and pull things apart. It's a throwback to primitive man; the wild ones, the reckless ones, they were the best hunters, the best warriors, the ones to breed with to ensure the survival of the tribe."

"Yeah, the ones with deep set eyes. Maybe we should squint more," mused Clancy. He squinted and jutted his chin forward but he just looked constipated.

For some reason I thought about the little girl who went missing from the next park down, a few years before. I wondered what could have happened to her. I wondered if she had been taken by some good-looking guy, a psychopath with an overhanging brow and deep-set eyes. I wondered what he could have done to her. I tried not to think about it. I tried not to think about all those little kids that get taken by bad men with overhanging brows. I thought; they must be frightened when they find out that the man is not a good man, not a kind man and that they are a long way from home.

"Squint, go on. I'll let ya know if it's an improvement," demanded Clancy. I squinted. "Yeah, mate irresistible!" He shoved me off the wreck and we swam back to shore, the cold water sharpening our senses.

"I'm goin' for a walk," I said.

"Okay," said Clancy "Nothin' else to do." He picked up a green piece of glass, masquerading as a shell, its sharp edges worn smooth by the shifting sand, and he skimmed it across the calm surface of the water. We watched it bounce, transfixed for a moment.

"Nah, I can't think when you're around, ya mouth just goes all the time. Ya think with ya mouth open. I don't know how ya do it." He looked offended.

"I don't think about thinking!" he blurted out. He stared at me. "What the hell are ya gonna think about?"

"I don't know! I don't know until I get started, then it just goes from there."

"From where?"

"From my head! I dunno! Fish! I'll probably think about fish. A man can learn a lot from fish."

"Yeah, who needs friends when you've got fish!" Clancy turned and walked back towards the caravans. He bent down and picked up a big wad of brown rubbery seaweed and flung it over his head, and I wondered how he knew I was watching him. Maybe he had some kind of sixth sense. I wondered what he thought about when he was alone in his own mind, not that he was ever alone much.

In the distance I saw a glint of silver hair; the girl was up early that morning walking towards us. As Clancy walked towards her, his head was a leathery bronze tangle of idiocy. He didn't even think to take it off, and when their paths crossed, she just stopped and laughed and turned to walk back to camp with him.

As I walked in the opposite direction, my head drifted from one thing to another, then back to Gilly and the fact that she was from the country and I was from the city, and that maybe we didn't have a lot in common. I thought I might try and impress her with big city slicker talk about how sophisticated my life was, what with all the art galleries, theatres and music venues just at the end of my street. I thought I might make up a pantheon of interesting, artistic friends, when the fact was, I spent most days alone with my computer tracking down conspiracy theories, descending into the holy rabbit hole of half-truths.

I'd tailgate traumatising tales of extraterrestrials, lizard men and greys; interplanetary beings who piloted the psyches of politicians and world leaders. I'd dragnet dastardly deeds done in paedophile pizza parlours. I went to places where lunatics lampooned lunar landings and talked of nine-foot Neanderthals nesting in the Antarctic. There were posts about Dionysian devotees dancing in Bohemian woods. It was a place where Satan's servants sacrificed their sanity and wars were preplanned, where the harpies of HARP warped the weather and control freaks fraternised with fate and fertility, pathologising population control.

Déjà vu? Déjà vu? I'd been there before, hundreds of

times and at the end of the day, I'd claw my way out of Alice's brave new world, where there was no rabbit to guide the way, and lost souls surrendered to a warp that stole their time; their lives. I'd come up gasping for air, just like the time I almost drowned at the wreck and Clancy saved me.

The hiccup of a motor boat, coming back from a fishing trip, nudged me back to reality and the memory of the fact that my parents had just broken up. I imagined that Mum had probably stayed up all night thinking about Dad and waiting for me to come back. I turned around and headed home to face the music. I couldn't help thinking that I probably had some sort of hand in the disaster, but I couldn't figure out what it was. The truth was, I had always tried to divide my loyalties fairly evenly between my parents, generally taking the side of whoever was the least absurd on any given day. Either way, I was always pretty sure that I was the closest thing to an adult in our house.

I expected Mum to be red-eyed and frazzled, but there she was, perky as a parrot, cheerily sipping tea on her sun-lounge; "Beautiful sunrise. Did ya catch it?" she asked.

"Yeah, me and Clancy watched it come up over the wreck."

"Thought you might be down there." She didn't seem even vaguely perturbed by the fact that our world had just tilted on its axis.

"Are you okay? Did you get any sleep?" I tried to broach the subject.

"Yep, went straight to bed and slept like a log."

Whereas Mum usually liked nothing more than to have a good whinge about Dad, on that particular day she avoided the topic like the plague.

Gilly's Dad

One night every summer, there would be a full moon. Sometimes it was big and red, and at other times it was like a massive gold coin sitting high in the sky, but more often than not, it was a sharp silver orb, which lent an eerie silver glow to the bay, and set the mighty wheel of the wreck in stark silhouette against a silvery sky.

One night that summer, that special summer, I was standing on the rocks staring up at the moon, when a cold shiver surged up my spine. I looked out at the wreck and saw something move on the wheel. I shrugged it off, thinking it was just the stray seal that used to sleep there sometimes, but the more I looked, the less it seemed like a seal. I watched a slim silhouette climb sure footed until it reached the top of the wheel.

She stood there, still as a statue, her hair glinting silver in the moonlight. 'It's now or never,' I thought and waded into the water, barely conscious of the stingrays and banjo-sharks darting over the sea floor. How many hundreds of times had I swum out to the wreck? I heaved myself onto its rusted hull, then picked my way across the frame, careful not to slice myself on mussels or the jagged metal outcrops. I climbed up the rungs of the wheel until I balanced on the rim next to her. She didn't say a word, she just sat down on the rim and gazed out at the silver-crested waves below. Time inched by in silence.

As I stared down at the silvery swell, it was as if it started to turn yellow, and the movement of the sea became the soft swaying of fields of buttery yellow flowers caressed by a warm breeze.

"What are you thinking?" she asked.

"Yellow, a field of yellow flowers, maybe sunflowers," I answered.

"No, it's canola. My father grew it and I danced through it as a kid. All that yellow made me laugh. I felt like my heart would burst. I was so happy, swirling in yellow."

As I gazed out at the yellow expanse, I thought I heard thunder, something that sounded like distant thunder, maybe a storm on the other side of the bay. Then I heard a harsh rustling sound and a great black cloud rolled over the fields, blotting out the sun, turning day into night, and night into black nothingness. I shivered.

"What are you thinking?" asked the girl.

"A cloud, a writhing black cloud, all the bright yellow

flowers are gone."

"Locusts, they wiped us out, destroyed the entire crop. It nearly broke him. I saw my dad sobbing in my mother's arms."

I didn't say anything. I didn't know what to say. I didn't know how to stop someone else's pain. I didn't even know if I wanted to hear about her life, the life she must have led outside of the here and now.

When I came to think of it, I didn't know much about anyone's life outside of the caravan park, outside of summer. I guessed they all lived somewhere, went to school somewhere, worked somewhere. All those other lives, those other selves, they seemed private. I never asked anyone about anything outside of Indented Head and no one ever asked me. There were times when I'd look at someone and wonder who they were and what they did, but I figured most of the kids were living lives much the same as mine, and no one wanted to talk about school on the holidays; but things had changed a bit that summer. One day I'd seen Clancy and the girl walking together to the jetty. They seemed to be laughing a lot, like they had a lot in common, which made sense, since they were both from the country. When Clancy came over to my van later that day, I asked him what he'd talked to her about. He said, "Nothing, just Ballarat."

"What about Ballarat? You never talk to me about Ballarat!"

"Nothing. Stuff that wouldn't interest you. She's a good listener."

"Sometimes I think I don't know anything about

you," I said.

"You know everything about me. I don't have to tell you stuff, you know who I am," said Clancy, matter-of-factly.

I stared out to sea and listened to the soft lap of silver waves against the hull of the wreck.

"Anything else?" the girl asked.

I didn't answer, I just kept listening to the lapping sound until the soft laps became sharp cracks. The waves weren't any bigger, just the sound grew sharper, more insistent, like the distant crackle of something burning. There was the smell of smoke, as if someone had lit a camp fire on shore, then the sound of explosions. like bombs going off in a distant war zone.

"Explosions," I said.

"Gum trees; the sap and the eucalyptus oil sound like explosions when they catch fire. After five years of drought, the fires came raging through the bush surrounding our farm. A farmer on the property next door was out rounding up a few cattle and didn't have time to get back to his house. He survived by killing one of the cows. He slit it open right down the middle and hauled the guts out of its belly, then crawled inside the carcass just before the flames passed over him. The wind carried the sparks into our wheat fields, which were already too dry, and burnt them to a black, flat waste. Dad didn't cry, he didn't speak, he just stared. He went silent."

"I'm sorry." It was the best I could do. I tried harder, "Your dad must have worked hard. It must have hurt to lose it all. All that hard work for nothing." She didn't say anything. She just stared out to sea.

I felt the first drops, big cold drops of rain, on my neck and shoulders. I watched rivulets run down her arms. She stuck out her tongue to catch a big droplet. I wished my tongue was close to hers. I lost track of time as thunder rumbled in the distance. The rain poured down, sharp and cold, stinging our skin. The wind whipped the waves into a mighty swell that beat against the hull of the wreck.

"Better get back," she said, and let herself slip off the wheel. I jumped in after her. The wind whipped around us as we shivered onto the shore.

"I know a place," I said, and grabbed her hand to pull her up the slippery cliff face to the empty caravan. I wedged open the side window next to the door, slipped my arm in and un-snibbed the lock, then slowly edged the door open, half expecting a vampire to leap out and suck me dry, but nothing out of the ordinary happened. There was just a sort of musty dank smell, like rotting chip board, as we stepped inside. I tried the light switch but there was no electricity. Gilly pushed back a curtain and a little ray of moonlight spilled in, just enough for us to see that the place was empty. We even tried the cupboards, but all the cups and pots and cutlery had been cleared out. The only trace of the old couple, who had once treasured the place, was a funny old floral bed cover. We wrapped it around our shoulders and huddled together on the bed to keep warm, while we listened to the rain pelting on the roof outside and felt the caravan sway with each gust of wind.

"You can smell rain," she said. "You can smell it coming; animals can smell it, insects can smell it. It's worse after a drought because you want it so much. It's like an act of kindness can break you once you've steeled yourself against the hard times. Once you've given up hope nothing can hurt you anymore, but the kindness of rain, it's like hope, it can break you."

"Yeah, like kindness. I guess so," I mumbled as I listened to the rain's sharp echo on the tin roof. The branch of an overhanging tree scrapped back and forth like the claws of some crazed animal trying to get in, but it didn't seem to bother Gilly, she just kept talking.

"Insects can sense rain. One morning, when I was a kid, I woke up and I thought that I could smell it, but when I ran outside everything was white like snow, as if it had snowed all night. I ran out into it until I was waist deep, thinking I would cool myself down, but it was thick and sticky. Hundreds of spiders were crawling and writhing up my legs. My mother screamed from the veranda, 'Get the hell out of there, they'll eat you alive!' I ran screaming back to the house, slapping the spiders off my legs as I ran. Mum tore my clothes off and shoved me under the shower, scrubbing me down with soap but I was still a mass of red welts the next day. You see, during the night, the spiders had made thousands of webs; a massive silver escape route. Mum said she had only seen it once before, when she was a girl, and that it only happened before a flood. Then we heard the first big splashes on the tin roof of our house. It rained and it rained. It turned those black, burnt paddocks into muddy swamps."

"It's like The Four Horsemen!" I exclaimed.

"No, there weren't any horsemen out there. We did

have a few sheep but Dad had taken them to higher ground the week before."

"No, not those kinds of horsemen, I meant The Four Horsemen of the Apocalypse. They're supposed to be Pestilence, Famine, War and Death, but I guess for farmers it'd be Pestilence, Drought, Floods and I don't know what the fourth one would be. Maybe it's Death, maybe it's just death."

Gilly took in a jagged little breath, then said, "My dad died."

It wasn't what I was expecting. I turned my head slowly to meet her gaze, but she wasn't looking at me, she was staring at some image she had conjured in the motley warn out lino on the floor. "He hung himself in the barn. I guess it all got too much for him. He left a note saying he was worth more dead than alive; insurance. I found him there, just hanging, his feet swaying gently, his face all blue."

She didn't cry or anything, and her voice was sort of hollow, as if all her feelings had drained away and she was just numb. I didn't know what to say, but for the first time since I'd met her, I felt like I could understand why she was the way she was; why she was so still and sad sometimes. I thought of her dad just hanging there.

She was quiet for a long time. Then she asked, "What happened out there on the wreck? It was like you were reading my mind?"

"I don't know. Maybe it's like my mother always says, 'Indented Head isn't so much a place as a state-of-mind.'"

As Gilly rested her head against my shoulder, I

breathed in the scent of her skin. "You smell like sea and honey," I whispered.

Gilly smiled, "That's funny because Mum used to keep a few bee hives. She used to sell honey in little jars at the local market. I'd to go with her and give it to people on little sticks, so they could try it. People say the bees are dying out in some areas and if they die, we die. I'm frightened there won't be enough of them to pollinate all the crops we need. Last year at school we read about some place in China where all the bees have disappeared, so the farmers pollinate the pear orchards by hand using feather dusters. They collect the pollen from one tree, on the end of a duster, then shake it out onto another tree. There was a picture of dozens of workers up ladders waving dusters into the branches. Mum told me that some farmers here are moving whole hives from one area to another area, so they can pollinate with less bees."

I was in heaven, lying in a caravan on a stormy night with a beautiful girl who smelt like honey. "I like bees," I whispered and brushed my lips across her hair. "I mean, I like the hum they make. I got bitten on the foot once when I was a kid. My whole leg swelled up, so my mother said I'd have to get it amputated. I told her I didn't want to get it amputated because I wouldn't be able to kick a footy. She said I'd just have to rise above it and become a paralympian."

Gilly started to laugh, "Your mum's a bit weird."

We stayed there the whole night, just talking and listening to the rain and doing what others must have done on stormy summer nights when there was nowhere else to go and when the fear of ghosts and vampires had been conquered. When we opened the door the next morning, there was Clancy, sitting on a rock just outside, staring at me.

"You didn't come home all night. Ya mum was worried. There was a storm."

"I know, we waited it out here."

"You could have gone home," Clancy growled and scowled.

"Well, we didn't."

"What were you doing?"

"Nothing. We weren't doing anything," I stammered. I could feel Gilly standing behind me on the caravan step. I don't know what she was feeling but she didn't say anything.

Clancy looked hurt. "Did you push the skeletons off the bed?" he asked sarcastically. Then he just stormed off.

Tango

Gilly was unnervingly quiet as we walked hand in hand back home to our caravans. It was one of those perfectly calm golden-pink mornings, completely innocent of the previous night's elemental passion. Her hand fitted perfectly in mine; her slender fingers slipped softly between my own. I kept smiling, I couldn't stop smiling. I felt ridiculously cheerful. When I tried to look at her, she just smiled and turned her head away, maybe self-conscious, as if I had discovered something private about her, something she didn't want anyone else to know.

"Won't your nan be worried?" I asked, breaking the silence.

"No, it's still early, she'll probably be asleep. Besides, she's used to me wandering off and taking moonlight dips. Sometimes when I can't sleep, I get my sleeping bag and go and sleep outside on the sand. The sound of the waves sends me to sleep. Nan pretty much leaves me alone; she doesn't ask too many questions. She says it takes a while to get over losing someone you love."

"Your nan sounds sane, mine is completely off her nut. She came to live with us after my grandad died. She talks to herself and tries to make cups of tea by putting teabags in the toaster, and when Grandad was sick in hospital, she kept whacking him over the head, telling him to stop being lazy and to get up and make her a cup of tea, because he'd had enough sleep! How long has your nan been coming down here? I don't remember seeing her around."

"Just a couple of years. She took over the site after her friend got sick and couldn't cope with camping anymore. She loves it, loves all the people. She says she never gets lonely down here because there's always someone to chat to."

When I asked Gilly if her mum was coming down, she went quiet, like she didn't want to talk anymore. Then she just stopped walking and sat down on the sand. I was scared that her mum's story was going to be as painful as her dad's, but I had opened the flood gates and there was no turning back.

"After Dad died Mum didn't want to be alone, so we moved in with Nan but it didn't help much. Mum got more and more depressed, then one day she just left. Nan found a note on the kitchen table. Mum wrote that she couldn't bear it anymore and that she was going to take a long drive. She said that maybe she would go and look for Norman. You see, Mum had spent her whole life feeling guilty about this kid called Norman. He was her best friend's little brother and the three of them played together in the neighbourhood gang when they were kids. All the kids called Norman 'Wormy Man' because he liked to eat worms when he was little. They'd all yell 'Wormy Man, Wormy Man ya can't catch me' and he'd chase them until they reached home-base on the veranda. He always had to be the chaser.

But the game that made Mum feel guilty happened after Norman's mum bought a giant playground rocket from a big shopping centre. The place was getting a new one and advertised for someone to buy the old one. Norman's mum thought it would be a great joke to get it, so one day a truck arrived with a crane and lowered the rocket into their backyard. It towered over all the houses and had two levels. Norman and his sister put metal colanders on their heads so they looked like astronauts and the local paper took their picture.

Mum and her best friend and Norman spent hours playing in that rocket. They'd go on journeys to strange planets and meet strange creatures, and when they got bored, they'd slip inside the house and steal a carton of eggs out of the fridge, then climb to the top level of the rocket and pelt the kids next door with eggs. When it came to gang warfare the rocket kids had the edge. They could see over all the fences and knew everything that was going on in all the other backyards.

Sometimes they played on the ground floor, which they had turned into a cubby house, and that was where Mum's friend kept her dolls. Norman would always ask if he could play the role of the dad but his sister and Mum would always say, 'No we don't need anyone to be the dad, we're married to each other.' Then, Norman would ask if he could be the doctor and the girls would say that nobody was sick. Finally, Norman asked if he could be the rubbish bin man. His sister thought that was a good idea. The three of them decided that the rubbish would be collected on Thursdays, not real Thursdays, just pretend Thursdays. Every now and then Norman would knock on the door and say, 'It's the rubbish bin man. I've come to collect the rubbish.' His sister and Mum would yell, 'Go away Norman, it's not Thursday, it's only Monday!' When he knocked again, they'd say that it was only Tuesday or only Wednesday. When Norman knocked again, he was really happy because he knew that Thursday came after Wednesday but when he yelled, 'I've come to collect the rubbish,' the girls would yell back; 'Go away Norman, its Friday! It was Thursday yesterday and you forgot to come!'

Mum said that in their childhood world, it was never Thursday so Norman grew sadder and sadder at being left out. When he got a bit older, he ran away. Mum thinks he must have been about twelve. He left a note to say he'd gone droving. He never came back and the police never found him. Mum always felt that it was her fault and that it was the cruel 'Thursdays' that made him want to run away and go droving. She must have read me the poem 'Clancy of the Overflow' a million times."

Then Gilly recited her favourite verse right off the top of her head:

'In my wild erratic fancy visions come to me of Clancy
Gone a-droving 'down the Cooper' where the Western
    drovers go;
As the stock are slowly stringing, Clancy rides behind
    them singing,
For the drover's life has pleasures that the townsfolk
    never know.'

"Mum always said that one day she'd find Norman and say sorry."

When we got back to the caravan my mother was sitting on the sun-lounge outside waiting. She grinned amiably at Gilly and acted like nothing had happened, as if she was always up bright and early.

"Mum, this is G--Gilly." I stuttered.

"I know who she is. I've been chatting to her nan for the past two years." Then she turned her attention to Gilly. "You've got such lovely hair! I bet you're hungry. Would you like a cup of tea and some toast?"

"No Mum, she's got to get back. Her nan is probably worried."

"It's okay, I already talked to her last night. We were a bit worried when you two didn't come back but I told her you were probably just sheltering somewhere." My mother eye-balled me. "Somewhere like the empty caravan? I hope there weren't too many skeletons lying about."

My mother was a nightmare! She kept smiling at Gilly. She really delighted in the prospect that I might have a girlfriend. A few days before, she had taken to asking me if I was gay, telling me not to be shy about it and that I should just let it all hang out of the closet!

I kept telling her that I was not gay, and that Clancy didn't have a girlfriend, and Aaron didn't have a girlfriend and they weren't gay either. "Zeke's doing alright for himself. The girls seem to love him!" she taunted me.

"Yeah Mum, but Zeke's a 'Zee.' He's not quite human." I snapped back at her.

Mum handed Gilly a cup of tea and smiled at her with such affection that I thought she was actually going to thank her for spending time with me. "Ah young love, it's marvellous! It reminds me of when I first met Jesse's dad."

"That wasn't young love Mum, you were friggin' forty and Dad was fifty!" It was true, I had the oldest parents in the caravan park. My parents were as old as some kids' grandparents.

"Young love is young love no matter how old you are!" Mum retorted.

"That doesn't make any sense! Young love is young love because the people involved are young!" I tried not to yell. Gilly was beginning to look uncomfortable.

"Rubbish! Now let me tell Gilly how your father and I met," Mum insisted.

"No Mum, please!" But she was off and once she got started there was no stopping her. I cringed and silently prayed to the universe to make my mother lose her voice, or maybe give her an attack of non-verbal diarrhoea, but there were no benevolent angels on duty that day; Mum just kept prattling on:

"Well, we first met at a fancy-dress ball. During the day I kept trying to think of something to wear but nothing seemed quite right, but then it suddenly occurred to me that I could wear one of my old theatre costumes; the golden ballgown and feathered mask. It was the costume I'd worn for a play set during a South American dictatorship and which told the story of a beautiful peasant girl who joined a rebel movement and eventually became the mistress of the dictator. On the night of the grand ball, she dressed in a magnificent golden gown and bird mask and slit the dictator's throat! I have to say I received excellent reviews in the New York Times!" Mum paused for effect. Gilly looked at me and raised her eyebrows. She must have thought that Mum was making it all up.

"It's true," I mumbled. "She used to be an actress. Her stories are mostly true. She's got a scrap book to prove it." Then Gilly looked at Mum with such eagerness to hear more that it made me wince, and Mum had all she needed to keep the story going:

"Well, suitably dressed, I arrived at the ball and I spotted a friend, so I went over to see if he wanted to dance, but he wasn't in the mood and suggested I dance with the fellow sitting next to him. The man had a very erect posture and lovely playful brown eyes. He was dressed as some sort of Cossack and said, "I vill dance vith you." I thought he was putting on a very poor Russian accent, but as Jesse knows, his father talks like that all the time! Well, the strange German-Cossack and I danced all night and into the early hours of the morning, until we were exhausted. Finally he asked me if I would like to go and get a coffee. We were in Carlton, so there were plenty of places open in the early hours of the morning. When we walked into a café in our costumes, a few people stared but most people just ignored us; people in Carlton were always wearing weird stuff. When we sat down the Cossack asked if I would take off my mask. I, of course, had completely forgotten that he had no idea what I looked like, so I slipped it off and what did he do? He just stared at me as if I wasn't what he was expecting, or as if I was some sort of alien. Either way he said nothing. He may have been handsome but he wasn't the best conversationalist and his irritating accent made it difficult to understand what he was saying. We drank our coffee and I caught a taxi home. And it wasn't until I got home and looked in the bathroom mirror that I realized my face was completely green! Maybe it was the sweat from dancing or maybe the mask had just oxidized, but whatever dye was inside that mask had come off, and I was green, green, green! And that man had said nothing! He'd just let me sit in that café like a deranged avocado!

Mum stared at Gilly expecting some sort of response. At a loss for words Gilly muttered, "I'm sorry."

"Oh, no need to be sorry dear." Mum continued on, "I was studying Tango at the time, it's a dance that comes all the way from Argentina. Do you dance?"

Gilly shook her head, "Ah no, not much."

"Well then you really should learn! It's an excellent way to meet people. I've been trying to get Jesse to go to lessons for years. You could go together! It's always good to have a partner!"

"Mum stop, please. She doesn't live in Melbourne!"

"Oh, what a shame, you two would look lovely together on a dance floor. Anyway, where was I? Ah yes:

Every month, the dance school would host a Tango Ball and on one particular occasion I had arranged to go with a friend, but at the last minute she couldn't make it. Funnily enough she said that she had the phone number of the strange Cossack-German that I had danced with at the masked ball, so she suggested I call him. By this time six months had passed and I was quite sure he wouldn't remember who I was. Nonetheless, I rang the number and there it was, that voice with the peculiar German accent: 'Yes, vot do you von't?' it asked. I was so taken aback by the abruptness of his opening sentence that I forgot to mention who I was. I simply said, 'I've got to go to the Tango Ball tonight and I need someone to go with.' The voice replied, 'The Tango is a very difficult dance.' So I replied, 'That's beside the point! Can you come?' The voice replied, 'Alwight.' So I gave the voice the address and meeting time and promptly hung up. It was only after I had hung up that I realized that the annoying man had no idea who he was meeting! Later that night, when we met at the ball, he stared at me and said, 'Oh, it's you.'

'Of course it's me!' I snapped. 'Who else would it be?'

'Vot?' he said. He seemed to be struggling with English.

'It's not 'vot', it's what with a w,' I helpfully informed him.

'That's vot I said!' he growled back. I could see that there was no point in pressing the point, so I suggested that we stop talking and get on with dancing, and as luck would have it, he could dance a whole lot better than he could speak!"

"Mum, can we just leave it there?" I begged, but she

was on a roll and there was no putting on the brakes.

"Don't be silly, I haven't gotten to the best bit!" She eye-balled Gilly meaningfully, compelling her to keep listening. "He really was a very good dancer. Well, after the ball, I said goodnight, hopped into a taxi and went home and didn't give him a second thought.

What is truly extraordinary about this tale is that every month, no matter who I invited to come with me to the Tango Ball, they always cancelled at the last minute and I would have to call the peculiar German. He would always say the same thing in less than enthusiastic tones, 'Oh, it's you, alwight, I go.' After seven or eight months of these unplanned encounters, he invited me have coffee at his studio after the ball. Well, while I was sitting there sipping a cup of tea and chatting about my brilliant career, in particular about a telemovie that I had made, he suddenly leapt up, ran to his bedroom and came back with a picture of himself in bed with a beautiful woman, 'Look, this is me and my vife!' Well, I was gobsmacked! 'Your wife?' I asked. 'Yes,' he responded cheerfully. As you can imagine, I was horrified and thought that I might be implicated in some sort of incident of betrayal, or that the man was planning some sort of ghastly ménage à trois!"

"Menage a what?" I interjected. My mother paused briefly and rolled her eyes, as if I was the least sophisticated person on the planet, then without any explanation continued on:

'It's very broad-minded of your wife to let you go dancing with me every month,' I said, but my sarcasm was lost on him. 'Vy vould she mind?' he asked, genuinely perplexed. Well, there was no accounting for some people's marital arrangements! So I let the matter rest, but I did adopt a more formal attitude when we met at the next Tango Ball, and when he asked me what was wrong, I reminded him that he was married. 'Married? Vot makes you think I am married?' He seemed totally bewildered, so I reminded him of the photo he'd shown me of his 'vife.' Then he said; 'But that was from a student vilm. You vere talking about being in a vilm, so I showed you a voto of me in a vilm!' 'But you didn't tell me it was from a vilm!' I mimicked him in frustration. So then he said, 'I thought you vould know. I thought ve vere on the same vavelength!' The man was impossible! But each month I would call him and each month he would escort me to the Tango Ball. Finally, I invited him to my place for dinner."

"Mum stop, please!" I whinged and cringed. I'd heard it all before. It wasn't entertaining, it was embarrassing. But Mum was unperturbed. "Don't interrupt when I'm telling a story darling." She kept barrelling forward, oblivious to the detrimental impact her dumb story could have on my love life. I kept thinking that Gilly might deduce that if my parents were insane, I might suffer from the same impediment!

"Well of course we made love, and afterwards, when we were just lying in bed talking, that strange German started to relate his first sexual experiences:

'My first experience vos vith ah… horse.'

'A horse? That's disgusting!' I blurted out. I couldn't believe that he was telling me something so perverted! Any man who has had relations with a horse should keep the matter to himself! It certainly wasn't an appropriate topic on a first date!

'It's not so bad,' he said, 'lots of men do it.'

'They may do it in Germany but they certainly don't do it here!' I exploded.

'Don't be ridiculous! All men do it!' he insisted.

I was appalled! 'All men do not do it. You are a pervert! Get out! Get out of my bed! Get out of my house!' I yelled.

'It vos a long time ago! You are so narrow minded!' he yelled back and slammed the door on his way out.

Well, I sat in silence staring at the wall asking myself how I had gotten involved with someone so devoid of common decency! 'A horse?' I kept rolling the thought, the word, around in my mind. 'Horse?' 'Horse?' 'Whores!' Oh, no! He meant whores! I wrapped a sheet around myself and ran to the front gate screaming, 'Come back! Come back! Whores are okay!'

He turned and walked back, 'Vot made you change your mind?'

'Horse, I thought you said you had sex with a horse.'

He looked at me as if I was insane, 'A horse! Vy vould I have sex vith a horse? Are you mad?'

'It's you! You don't speak English properly!' I stammered. Then guess what?"

Mum looked at Gilly, expecting her to guess what came next. Gilly looked at me but I just stared at the ground.

"Nine months later Jesse was born! How's that for a love story!"

Mum had finally finished and my humiliation was complete. The good thing was, Gilly was laughing. I glared at Mum and grabbed Gilly's hand before Mum could embark on another one. "Come on, let's get you back to your nan."

When we got to Gilly's van, her nan looked at her calmly and said that she had been worried. "I gather you were in safe hands," she said.

The slightest glimmer of irony played beneath her cool, blue eyes. The clarity of her gaze was a far cry from the misty madness that clouded my own nan's gaze. I wondered how one person could grow old with such clarity and another sink below the surface of sanity. I knew with my nan it was an illness, a disease but some part of me believed that it had something to do with will; the will to be here. Maybe it had to do with curiosity, to see how the story ends. After Grandad died, Nan just wanted to slip away. She lost interest in her own story.

"And was she in safe hands, young man?"

I snapped out of it. Why did my mind wander so much? How long had Gilly's nan been staring at me? "Safe? Um safe. It was raining," I stammered lamely.

"Would you like a cup of tea?" she asked curtly.

Not tea again! Why did old ladies always offer you tea? What was in the stuff? I explained that I had to get back, and quickly slipped through the annex flap to the safety of blue skies, away from her prying eyes.

So nice you've got a girlfriend

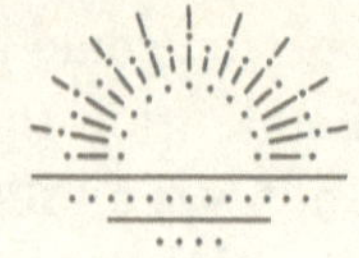

When I got back to the caravan, Mum was waiting for me; "It's so nice you've got a girlfriend! I'm so glad you're not gay! It's not that I don't love gay people, the theatre is full of gay people! I'm just glad about having grandchildren!"

"Mum, Gilly and I aren't planning on breeding anytime soon. We just met!" I tried to make my mother see reason. I tried to quell her irrational enthusiasm. I tried not to think about the possible consequences of my actions.

"But you never know! Sometime in the future ..." Mum kept prattling. That was the point I didn't know. "I always wanted a daughter, someone to chat to!"

"We chat! What do you call our conversations! I thought you talked to me about everything!" I exploded.

"Of course I do darling, but it's not the same, you're a male."

My mother was the most sexist person on the planet! I quoted her favourite words of wisdom; "The Y chromosome addles the brain!"

"Stop being silly and tell me all about it," she insisted.

"All about what?" I decided the best tactic was to play dumb.

"Your romantic evening." She smiled conspiratorially, "Are you still a virgin? It's not good to stay a virgin for too long. It rots your privates!"

"Mum, this is private! I'm not telling you anything! It's none of your business! You're impossible!"

"Don't be silly! I'm your mother!"

"Other people don't tell their mother everything!"

"Well, you don't have to be like everybody else! You don't have to be a sheep!"

"Yes I am!" I yelled, "I am a sheep! A very private sheep! Baa, baa." I stormed out of the annex with Mum following me shouting, "Come back! Sheep are okay!

Conversations

I spent the rest of the day wandering around the caravan park. I wanted to find Clancy and try to explain what had happened, but he wasn't anywhere to be found. He must have caught a lift to the surf beach. As I walked around, I let the crazy carnival of conversations wash over me.

I passed a woman sitting outside her van. She had her head in her hands. When she looked up, I could see she'd been crying and one eye looked pretty badly bruised. I don't know why I stared. "What're you staring at?" she snapped. Then a man came out of the annex and grabbed her by the arm and said, "Get inside, people will see ya." The woman pulled her arm away and said "I want them to see! I want them to see what you are." The man said, "'No one gives a shit," and hauled her back inside. I wanted to say that I gave a shit but I just kept walking, like everyone else. I imagined a few of us ambushing the guy one night at the urinal and having a few urinary accidents, or I thought we could misjudge a few cricket balls while he was sun baking on the beach. But I did nothing, like everybody else I did nothing.

On my way to the shop across the road to get a pie, I passed the professor with the short grey beard, who spent whole summers just reading and who always camped alone. He was in the phone booth because the mobile phone reception at the camping ground was so bad. I heard him say, "When it comes to destroying those historical statues, I say pull them down, there's a difference between recording history and glorifying bastardry!" Then he started pleading into the receiver, "Just come down for lunch, I promise not to compromise your chastity." I turned that line over and over in my mind, 'I promise not to compromise your chastity.' There were hundreds of possibilities; I wondered who she was, what their relationship was. I wondered why she didn't want to come down for lunch. I wondered why a man who liked being alone so much suddenly didn't want to be alone. I wondered why he didn't talk to anyone in the caravan park.

Later in the day, when I was sun baking on the wreck, I overheard Clancy's sister and another girl talking. It seemed an unlikely friendship given they looked so different. While Miranda had a classic girl-next-door look with her wavy light brown hair, glowing skin and hazel eyes, as mischievous as Clancy's; her friend had long, straight, dyed black hair with a short-cropped fringe, vampirishly pale skin and a sullen expression. She wore a ring in her nose and one in her left eyebrow, and her fingernails were painted black. Her deep purple lips seemed to emphasise her pain or shame as she spoke. She was showing Miranda all the little white lines and little red lines like scars running up one arm.

I pretended to be asleep or lost in my own thoughts. They didn't take any notice of me. Miranda and I had been ignoring each other since we were little. Whereas I found Clancy to be one of the most interesting people on the planet, his younger sister was just plain boring, but I listened in on her conversation anyway. It wasn't as if I had anything better to do.

"You ought to stop. It doesn't look good," said Miranda.

"I can't stop, it feels good when I do it," her friend answered.

"How can it feel good? It must hurt."

"Yeah, it hurts a bit at first, but it stops me thinking; I'm just there in the moment watching the blood seep out. It's like the physical pain stops the mental pain. I just stop feeling lonely for a while."

"But you're not lonely, you've got friends down here," Miranda comforted her.

"Yeah, but when I go back home, there's no one, I mean no one I like being with. They're all just really mean and bitchy at school; it's like I'm the local punching bag. Do you think I'm fat?"

"You don't look fat to me, just kind of normal, a bit

plump maybe, but not fat with a capital F."

"Plump! What's that supposed to mean?"

"It means, don't worry about it. Nobody down here cares what anyone looks like. Look at those oldies wading into the water, I mean they just let it all hang out."

"They're old!"

"It's not worth hurting yourself over. Can't you just ignore the bitchy bullies at school?"

"I can't ignore them, I'm their sport! Anyway, it's not as if I'm the only one who does it; there's this crazy little online community that shares shots of cuts, it's almost cool."

"Friggin' depressing if you ask me. What about your parents? They must know, they must see your arms."

"Mostly I keep my arms covered, but yeah, they know, I mean they've seen it. They know I do it but they don't say anything, they just act like it's not happening. They just act super cheerful. It's like if they don't notice, it will go away."

The girl caught me staring at her arm, "What's ya problem?" she snapped.

Miranda glared at me and stuck her middle finger up. I rolled off the wreck and into the salty water, sterilising what I'd seen and heard.

After dinner, as the sun was setting, I took another walk around the park, thinking that I might bump into Clancy, but he wasn't back yet. I strolled over to the barbecue area where I heard a couple of mums talking about their best friends:

"When my best friend got divorced, she'd call me

every night at ten o'clock, just before bedtime. I guess that was when she was feeling lonely and I'd console her. We'd talk for hours! I'd do impersonations of her ex-husband and she'd laugh until her belly ached! I got her through it. But years later when I got divorced and needed a little support, she said she wasn't interested and that she didn't have time to come over for a drink and a talk. She had completely forgotten about all the times I'd supported her. In fact it was one of my neighbours, that I didn't know half as well, who got me through it. She came over and in her lovely Yorkshire accent said, 'I know you're angry but you must be hurtin'. Why don't you come and have dinner with us tonight? From then on, she rang every Thursday night and invited me over for dinner. It went on for months."

"Oh, I know, I know," said the other woman. "When my boy had a skateboarding accident and couldn't walk for a year, and not one specialist could figure out why he was in such excruciating pain, my best friend was as mean-spirited as a person can be. At one point my boy hadn't talked to anyone his own age for months, so I asked her if she could get her son to come over to cheer him up. I mean the boys had been good friends when they were younger and I'd taken her boy on dozens of bike rides and picnics and horse riding. Do you know what she said? She said, 'Oh no, I couldn't do that, Micky is so busy with his sport and music, he wouldn't have the time.' Now if it was her child that was all alone and unable to walk, I would have told my son to get the hell over there. The thing is I wouldn't have had to force my son because he would have gone over there himself out of the kindness of his heart."

"It's funny about best friends," the other woman said, "sometimes they're just not worthy of the title, 'best'."

"Oh, I agree, I agree! Friends can be so disappointing. Sometimes people you barely know are a whole lot kinder."

I rolled the conversation over in my head as I lay in bed that night and thought about friendship. I thought about Clancy and wondered if I had betrayed him by taking Gilly to the empty caravan. I mean it wasn't as if he owned her, they weren't engaged, hell they hadn't even been on a date!

Jogging

The next morning the tide was in and the sun hid behind the clouds, casting a bluish haze over everything. I walked outside just in time to see Clancy jogging along the track on his way to the jetty. We'd done it a million times. There were a couple of years when all the guys were obsessed with fitness, so we'd all race to the jetty and back. The thing about sport or competing physically was, you didn't have to talk, you didn't have to make conversation. When we were about fourteen or fifteen, things went a bit awkward. Sometimes when we couldn't think of anything to say we'd just wrestle each other to the ground or race to the jetty. When he got a bit older the only time Clancy went running was when he was in a bad mood.

He'd already reached the boathouse before I pelted after him. Gasping for breath I caught up to him and we jogged in silence, at a nice steady pace.

"Where'd you go yesterday?" I asked.

Clancy picked up his pace, "I was busy."

"With what? Running the Scrabble championships?"

I was trying to be funny but he didn't appreciate it. The fact was, Clancy hated Scrabble. He just couldn't see the point of people sitting around cobbling words together for no good reason. One time, I remember telling him it was like sport; you didn't have to make conversation but you could still hang out with people. I told him that sometimes Scrabble was hilarious. He said that he'd never had a good laugh playing Scrabble!

Clancy didn't budge, he just kept jogging. We passed the jetty. He wasn't going to stop; he was going to make me haul it all the way to St. Leonards. Half way there he broke his silence, "Why'd ya do it? Why'd ya have to take her to the empty caravan? Why didn't ya just take her home?"

"There was a storm," I said lamely.

"Bullshit! It's not like it's a hundred kilometres from the wreck to her van!"

"Well, I didn't! We were talking."

"You could've talked at her place."

"Sure, with her nan offering us cups tea every ten minutes!"

"You didn't give me a chance."

"A chance to what? You had heaps of time talking to her about the joys of living in Ballarat!"

"That's just it, we have things in common. She's from the country. She doesn't like the city."

"Neither do I!" I lied. The fact was I loved it. I loved the sound of the trams rattling down High Street. I loved the smell of every country of the world wafting out from all the restaurants at the end of our street. Sometimes I'd take a walk and just breathe it all in; Greek kebabs, Italian lasagne, Indian curries, Korean barbecue, Vietnamese Pho. My stomach rumbled. I glared at Clancy, "Anyway, Gilly and me have other things in common."

"Like what?" demanded Clancy.

"Like not having brothers or sisters. Like not having a happy nuclear family. Like everything not being normal."

"Nuclear family? Why the hell do they call it a nuclear family? Sounds like it's going to explode and everyone's going to get radiation poisoning."

I thought of my parents' impending separation, "Yeah, that's exactly what happens."

"What else? What else do you two have in common?" demanded Clancy.

"Books. She likes reading books. She said her favourite book was Tess of the d'Urbervilles."

"Tess of the what?" snarled Clancy.

"Forget it. It's just a book she read. She said her favourite bit was when Tess was talking to some guy about important dates, like Christmas and birthdays, Australia Day, I don't know. Then the guy says that there is another important date lurking in the shadows, like a sly snake in the grass; the date of our death."

"Well, that's cheerful," snapped Clancy.

"Her dad died. Did you know?"

Clancy stopped running and caught his breath, "No, she didn't tell me that." We sat down under the cedars. The sweat poured down our faces as we soaked up the shade. "She didn't tell me that," he whispered.

We sat in silence for a while, then Clancy said, "Ya took advantage of her. You took advantage of her sadness." Then he got me in a headlock and tried to rip my head off. We kicked up the dust around us as we wrestled each other to the ground. When I finally broke lose, I yelled, "Use ya words Clancy! Use ya fuckin' words!" Then I stormed off back to camp with his words ringing in my ears; 'You took advantage of her sadness.'

A lawyer? A Fucking lawyer?

When I got back to the caravan, I slumped onto the sun-lounge and scowled out to sea. Mum cheerily bumbled out of the annex holding her perennial cup of tea. She was the last person I wanted to talk to. "What's up? I thought you were playing with Clancy," she chortled.

"We're not children, we don't play!"

"Well, whatever it is you people do … jog? Where's he been? I haven't seen him for a day or two."

"Where's he been?" I mimicked her voice. "He's been sulking."

"Why? Clancy's not the type to sulk."

"He's a dickhead," I snarled.

"Oh, so the bromance is over?" She smirked smugly.

"Bromance? Bromance! Do you have to use those dumb, pseudo cool expressions?"

"Well, I can see love doesn't agree with you. Where's Gilly?"

"I don't want to talk about Gilly!" I snapped."

"You want to talk about Clancy?"

I heaved a sigh. I felt exhausted. "No, no. I don't want to talk about anyone."

"In other words, Clancy's jealous. He's hurt because you got the girl. I see things. I notice things."

"Well good for you! The all-knowing, all-seeing eye of Horace!"

"Oh, you are clever!" Then Mum came over and gave me a kiss on the forehead. She was so patronising! I hated her! Somehow, I felt like it was all her fault. "Don't worry, he'll get over it. There's plenty of fish in the sea."

"There aren't plenty of fish in sea! If industrial fishing continues at its current rate, there won't be any fish in thirty years! And there aren't plenty of girls like Gilly in the sea."

Mum blithely ignored my frustration "The funny thing is, I would have thought that a girl like Gilly would have gone for Clancy. They're both from the country you know."

"Of course I know they're both from the friggin' country!" I spat out.

"You're just in a bad mood because you don't know what you're doing or where you're going. Your life lacks direction." Mum continued to poke the bear.

I stared at the sky. 'Oh, God help me,' I thought, 'I think I'm going to kill my mother!' Then inspiration struck; "Law, I'm going to study law. I'm going to be a lawyer."

In that instant the world stopped spinning, the breeze stopped blowing and the sun hid behind a cloud. The waves stopped waving and my mother's face froze as her mouth gaped open. I felt the earth's tremor. My mother's sneezes were the cathartic release of demons. They began with a gasp of air, followed by a high-pitched buzzing sound, as if a bee was caught up her nostril. She tried to stifle the explosion by clamping her lips shut. Then it burst forth with the blood curdling screech of a banshee. Two more of the same magnitude followed. My mother always sneezed in threes. Then the tirade began:

"A lawyer? A fucking lawyer! Scumbags and psychopaths! Control freaks and fraudsters, who think they're above the law! Power hungry profiteers! Do you have any idea how much some of those conniving creeps charge people to settle their divorces or separations?" I just shrugged, there was no point arguing. "Why can't you do something useful, like being a plumber, or an electrician, or a brickie! Why can't you be someone who builds something rather than one of those bullshitters who just pulls things down, and over charges for the privilege!"

My mother had obviously forgotten her previous tirade against brickies at the beginning of that summer. At least she hated everybody equally, and in that moment, turned her loathing to lawyers. The fact was, there was only one occupation I could do that would please her and that was becoming a writer. The problem was, I wasn't so sure I wanted to please my mother.

I remembered when I was about twelve, I told my parents that I needed to speak to them. I was furious with them and blurted out that they should be ashamed of themselves because they were financially illiterate. My mother pursed her lips and mimicked 'financially illiterate'. The two of them burst out laughing and said that it was probably true. When I asked them what they were going to do about it, they just laughed even harder and said that I would have to support them when they were old. This made me even more furious, so I reminded Mum that she had been engaged to a corporate lawyer for a few years when she was in New York. I said, "You should have married him, then we'd be rich!" Mum was hysterical and spluttered, "But darling if I had married the New York lawyer, you wouldn't exist!"

I tossed the idea of having a different father around in my head. The fact was, I couldn't be exactly sure that I had a firm grip on the workings of the universe. I couldn't be sure that I would still have been me if I'd had a different father. When I asked Mum why she didn't marry the lawyer and become rich, her answer was simple; "I didn't love him." In the end I conceded that it was probably a good thing that she had conceived me with Dad, but sometimes in the middle of the night, I wondered who I might have been, if she'd bred with somebody else. In the meantime, I decided to stick with the plan to be a lawyer. It was probably worth it just to see Mum totally exasperated.

I made my escape. I grabbed my goggles and snorkel

and headed for the wreck. The sunlight played on the water casting hexagonal honeycomb patterns on the sandy sea floor. The patterns looked like the synaptic pathways of the human brain. It felt like the sea was one big pulsating brain, as swimmers slipped across its surface, ignorant of its mind.

Zara and Gilly

It was a perfect Indented Head dusk, no wind and the wreck was a muted mirage in a hazy pink glow. The sea was soothingly still as we walked along the sand banks towards Portarlington. The pelicans nodded as we passed, sagely signalling their approval of young love.

"I saw you talking to Zara. I knew you two would get on," I broke the silence.

"Yeah, I like her."

"What did you talk about?"

"I don't know, just stuff, girl stuff. You know, like, who likes who."

"Whoo whoo likes whoo?" I hooted.

"Well, Alexis likes Shelton but Shelton likes Miranda. Miranda likes Gus but Gus likes Lucy. Lucy likes Nelson but Nelson likes Kelly. Hope likes Bryce and Bryce likes Hope."

"Yeah, it's a marriage made in heaven. And who does Zara like?"

"Zara likes Clancy but Clancy likes …." Gilly went silent and looked at the sand.

"Gilly, but Gilly likes Jesse," I finished her sentence for her.

Gilly laughed. "So now I'm with you, Zara and I can be friends. I liked talking to her. We walked all the way to St Leonards and back."

"What else did you two talk about?"

"Well, she wanted to know if I was okay, really okay after the bike ride. She said that the guy who jumped on me was a prick and a coward, and that she was sorry for not doing more to help. She said that when he pushed me to the ground, she just froze. She said that I should find out who he is and lay charges against him, because it was assault."

"Is that what you want to do?" I asked. "Maybe that's what you should do." Gilly hesitated. She wasn't comfortable. I had stumbled into girls' territory. Maybe it was none of my business. I waited.

"If I did something it would just cause a big fuss and everyone would know, and everyone would stare at me or try not to stare at me. I don't want to talk to the police. Besides, in the end nothing happened. Clancy humiliated him. That dickhead is going to question the size of his penis for the rest of his life. With any luck, he'll be too ashamed to ever take it out again. Maybe that's enough, maybe I should just let it go."

I bent down and picked up a small grey crab and gave it to Gilly. I didn't know what to say. I didn't know what to think. In fact I had avoided thinking about it. No one talked about it. It all happened so quickly that no one really knew what happened, except Gilly.

"I know what you're thinking. You're thinking that I'm a coward and that if he did it once he could do it again, and that I should tell the police so it doesn't happen to someone else, but I can't."

I put my arm around her shoulders. "Did you tell your nan?"

"Of course not. She'd get too upset." Gilly pulled away. "Did you tell your mum? You seem to tell her everything."

"Of course not. I don't tell her everything. She'd probably make things worse. She'd probably organize a posse of mothers to patrol Edwards Reserve for the rest of the summer."

"So no one told?"

"A couple of the kids just said some baddies had chased them. It's up to you, no one will say anything if you don't want them to."

"I don't want to say anything and I don't want to do anything, and I don't want to feel that helpless ever again."

A light breeze scattered her hair across her face and for an instant she looked like she was wearing a silvery Venetian mask. For the slightest moment she was someone I didn't know. When I looked ahead, I could see that the sandbanks were slipping away, as the sea surreptitiously lapped at their edges.

"C'mon, let's go back, the tide's starting to come in." I took her hand and we walked for ages in silence. I kept thinking how good it was to be able to walk with someone and not have to talk. The only other people I could do that with were me, myself and I. The only time Clancy was silent was when he was pissed off and his silence was deafening. Gilly bent down and picked up a lump of Neptune's necklace and started pulling off the rubbery pearls, leaving a trail behind us, a bit like Hansel and Gretel leaving breadcrumbs. I guessed that if we ever wanted to find our way back to that conversation, we'd only have to follow Neptune's pearls, that's if the tide didn't wash them away. I tried to shift the subject. "So, how's Zara going?"

"She's worried about her dad. She thinks he's becoming unhinged." I started laughing. It was the word 'unhinged,' it always made me and Clancy laugh. We were always accusing each other or someone of being 'unhinged.' It was our word, so it was strange to hear it coming out of Gilly's mouth.

"I think if people aren't already unhinged when they get down here, after a few seasons the salt air begins to rust their hinges."

Gilly smiled and kissed me. "No, Zara's really worried. Her dad keeps yelling, 'Souls can wait, seas can't.' She said that one day he got his note book out and started listing each kid's future occupation. He said his generation was lost and that saving the planet was up to the next generation. So, Zeke has to become an environmental scientist, Zed has to become a marine biologist, Zeth has to become a park ranger,

Zeb has to become a physicist, Zara has to become an environmental lawyer. On and on he went, allocating their careers and any Zee leftover has to become an environmental activist."

Years later, I remember catching a glimpse of Zara on the news. She was with a group of climate activists, and they had all glued themselves to the middle of a main road in the CBD, right at morning peak hour. It drew a lot of attention to the issue of climate change but it also made a lot of people angry because it made them late for work. I had to admire her courage and conviction and her faith in the fact that no one would accidentally or deliberately run them over, but I also wondered if the anger it caused didn't overshadow the cause. When I saw her again the following summer, I told her that I had been worried about her leaving great chunks of skin stuck to the road when the police dragged her away. She just laughed and said that they simply dissolved the glue with acetate, that stuff in nail polish remover, so I shouldn't worry about her too much and that there were more important things to worry about.

"Zara said that the other night, she found her dad sitting on the edge of the jetty with his fishing rod in his hand, silently crying, whispering to the fish he'd caught then throwing them back into the water."

"Do you think she's the closest one to him?" I asked. "There's so many of them, I wonder if he ever gets time to talk to any of them as individuals or whether they're all just part of the pack."

"Zara said that she gets some time alone with him because she almost always goes out surfing with him in the mornings, to catch the 6 a.m. swell. She said there's a lot of surfies up at that hour. Even if they've had a big night, they drag themselves out of bed and let the surf wash the haze from their brains. She said when they've had enough of the surf, they sit on the sand for a while and Zara listens while they talk to her dad. They talk about not being able to get a job, or breaking up with their girlfriend, or some bad decision they've made. She said her dad just listens. He doesn't preach on the beach. Zara thinks some of them just seem a bit lonely."

We'd almost reached the caravan park and when we were almost opposite the wreck, Gilly sat down in the sand and stared out to sea. "Sometimes I worry about my mum. I worry about her being lonely. She went nuts after Dad died. Then she just drove off to look for that kid who isn't a kid anymore, someone who could be dead, who knows. She's been gone almost a year. She sends a text message now and then or sometimes a letter. I keep saying I could meet her somewhere but she just keeps saying she wants to be alone. Dad used to say it takes four seasons to know whether you've made the right decision or not, and four seasons for grief to heal. Nan picked up a letter from the post office the other day. Mum writes one letter at the beginning of each season."

"What did she say? What did your mum say? Is she coming home?" I asked Gilly. I knew that if she had her mum to talk to, she wouldn't feel so bad.

"Do you want to see the letters? I could read them to you." The idea of reading her mum's letters seemed to make Gilly happy, so I said yes and we wandered over to her place. I was glad her nan wasn't there. She must have been out having cups of tea somewhere. We squished into the bench-seat behind the table and Gilly unfolded the first letter.

Letters

Hi Darling,

Sorry for leaving in such a hurry, not sure what came over me, some sort of panic attack I guess. I just had to get away. Don't worry about me, I'm okay and things are sort of interesting on the road. It's so hot here. I'm writing from a place called Denman. I know what you're thinking; where the hell is that? Somewhere in N.S.W. and don't ask how I got here, I just followed the rumours about a boy and here I am. Someone who seemed to fit Norman's description came up here looking for work on the farms decades ago. I don't know why he didn't just pick oranges in Mildura. I don't understand his movements, they don't make sense or maybe I'm just following fantasies. It was all such a long time ago. It doesn't matter, I just want to tell you about someone I met. I stopped at a café to have some lunch and you won't believe this, I started to chat to an old lady at the next table. She must have been in her eighties. At first, I thought she must have had a touch of dementia because she just stared into her teacup and kept stirring it with her teaspoon. The owner of the café came over and offered to make her a fresh cup, saying that hers must be cold. Then he looked at me and said, 'This is Maggie. She comes in most days for a cuppa and a chat, don't ya love?' Maggie nodded and the café owner said that Maggie had been a bit low lately on account of the drought and the state of her orange trees. The old lady sparked up and said that they were a hundred years old; older than her and that they had never died before, never in a hundred years! Well, we just kept talking and she told me about her life on the farm and then she ended up inviting me to come out to see her orange trees. She even said I could stay the night. I think she must have been a bit lonely. So, I ended up saying yes, and drove out there. My God, Gilly, you should have seen those orange trees! They were ancient and withered and wondrous. We walked along row after row of tortured trunks, their bare, gnarled branches reaching to the sky, begging for rain. The old woman patted each one as we passed. The dry, wrinkled, spotted skin on the back of her hands was almost an exact replica of the bark on those trees. I thought that if she stripped off her clothes and stood perfectly still, frozen in time, she'd become one of them and wither and die alongside them. Then, just as I was imagining her as an ancient orange tree, she turned around and grumbled that it was the bastards upstream, the cotton growers and the rice growers, taking more than their fair share of water, who were drinking the basin dry. She said that the water authority was full of useless bastards and that they needed to change the water allocations to leave more flow in the river system so that things didn't get too salty. She got really angry and asked me why we were growing cotton. She said, 'That's the kind of thing Americans do.' Then she insisted that we're too dry to be growing rice and that we weren't in 'bloody Asia.' I was going to argue the geographical point but thought it might be best to let it go. She worked herself up into such a state that she started to cry. I think trying to run a farm at her age was all a bit much, so I put my arms around her tiny shoulders and she sobbed, big loud, dry sobs as if there wasn't enough water in her body to make tears. I cried too because I kept thinking about your dad and how the drought broke him and because I miss him so much. That night, when we were eating dinner, the old lady asked me why I was there, so I told her that I was looking for Norman. She said that a lot of blokes had passed through over the years during picking season and that he could have been one of them. She said most of the ones she had known had moved North to work on cattle stations or the mines. I guess I'll head North tomorrow.

Love you.

Mum.

It was getting pretty dim in the caravan by that time. The familiar smell of frying onions and sausages wafted through the window and my stomach rumbled. Gilly flicked on a light switch and beamed at me as she reached up and grabbed a packet of biscuits from the

242

cupboard. "Don't suppose you want a cup of tea?" she asked. "Nah, can't stand the stuff," I said.

Her mother's letter had made her happy and for some dumb reason the image of the old lady's hands being like the bark of an orange tree made me happy. We sat there grinning at each other. "Do you want to hear another one?" she asked and I nodded. I loved listening to her voice and watching the concentration on her face as she read.

Hi Darling,

Hope you and Nan are managing okay. I'm up here in Mackay and all anyone is talking about is a big new coal mine being opened up in the Galilee Basin. I'm staying at a nice little hotel, but last night when I went downstairs for dinner, a fight broke out. The locals are truly divided. Some of them think that the new mine will create lots of new jobs, while others argue that it won't create more than a few hundred jobs and even those jobs could go to outsiders. Some farmers are saying that the mine could affect the water supply, because digging down to reach the coal seam could displace enough water to reduce pressure in the underground aquifers and stop the flow in local springs. Farmers downstream from the mine site are worried, and the ones who rely on the Carmichael River are concerned that if the mine uses too much water, the river will become too acidic and salty. One woman was yelling that her husband needed a job, while another woman was screaming that the mine would destroy wildlife habitat and decimate species like the black-breasted finch. The other woman's husband yelled that he didn't give a stuff about bloody black-breasted finches. He didn't see the point in saving bloody birds when his own family was going to starve to death because he didn't have a job. Then someone else started yelling about Point Abbott being dredged so big coal ships could come in, which would lead to all the sediment smothering sea beds for hundreds of kilometres. Someone else said that all the dredged muck would be dumped in the wetlands which would destroy even more habitat. The two husbands of the women started bumping up against each other. Then one shoved the other bloke's beer glass off the table and started shouting that the bloody mine was going to destroy the Great Barrier Reef and with it the Queensland tourist industry, so just about everyone would be out of a job! Then his wife backed him up and started chanting 'coal is dead,' and half the pub joined her in the chant. When that died down, a man with a very quiet voice, who didn't seem to be from around those parts, said that investment in coal had plummeted and that even banks and insurance companies were getting out. Then one of the women screamed that if the coal industry continued everyone would be unemployed because everyone would be dead! Then the other woman leant over and slapped her face. One thing led to another and pretty soon they were pulling each other's hair and scratching each other's faces. And all the while a cute little ukulele trio was in a corner playing 'You Are My Sunshine'. I have to say it was a great night and I've never learned so much in such a short amount of time. I might even take up the ukulele when I get back home. Over the next few days I tried to get a lead on Norman, but all I could find out was that most of the men who had passed through years ago had probably found work on the sugar cane farms.

Promise me you'll come up and see the Great Barrier Reef one day, before it gets destroyed.

Love you,

Mum.

Gilly lifted her head and looked at me, waiting for a response. I shoved the last biscuit into my mouth and chewed it, deliberately, thoughtfully, as I played for time. It was one of those soft shortbread biscuits with jam in the middle, the kind that old ladies like to eat, the kind that definitely needs to be washed down with something. With the last biscuit semi-lodged in my throat, I spluttered "She sounds great, your mum, she notices things. She's a really good writer. Maybe she should learn the ukulele, it might cheer her up. Are there any more?"

Gilly stared at the empty packet. "Biscuits?" she asked as if she'd never seen a healthy male devour a whole packet of biscuits in five minutes flat before.

"No, letters," I laughed and coughed at the same time. "Are there any more letters? Where did she go next?"

Gilly flicked through the letters but she couldn't find the one she was looking for. "In another letter, Mum wrote that she made it all the way to Townsville up north, just before it flooded. When the rains began, they went on for days. The main street became a river. From her hotel window, she saw a car float past. When the floods subsided, she asked around town to see if anyone had known of a man called Norman, but people were too preoccupied with the clean-up to pay Mum much attention. She finally found someone who said that a drifter had passed through a while back, who told him he'd been droving since he was a kid, but lots of drifters had passed through over the years. It was nothing new."

Then Gilly paused and gazed out of the window as she tried to recall where her mother had gone to next. She closed her eyes and knitted her brows together as if she were playing an imaginary film of her mother's journey inside her head. Then her beautiful grey-green eyes fluttered open and she smiled. "Now I remember, she said weeks later, travelling back south, she'd seen Lake Eyre come alive. She'd arrived at just at the right time. She called it, 'a once in a lifetime experience.' The dry lake had flooded and flocks of birds flew overhead, while pelicans paddled on the shore and a whole garden of pink algae floated on the surface of the perfectly still waters. She said she felt like she was on another planet. She described it so precisely that I could see it in my head and the funny thing was, when she finally sent me a photo, it was almost exactly the same as what I had imagined. Then in the same letter she talked about passing through Bourke just after the bushfires had raged through. People were pretty shaken up and no one wanted to talk to a stranger, they had their own worries, but she finally found an old resident who remembered that decades earlier a boy had worked on a few properties around those parts, but then he'd shot through. It was nothing new. A few days after that, she ended up in a place called Menindee, where the river was swollen with dead fish. The stench made Mum vomit her guts out and she said that she wondered if the Darling River was anybody's darling. She said she found out that a young man, who could have been Norman, had worked in the area years and years ago. They said he had gotten a girl pregnant, then skipped town. They said that sort of thing happened now and then, it was nothing new."

"Sounds like your mum's been through a lot. She must be exhausted," I said. The fact was, I was feeling pretty tired myself for no good reason other than I wasn't used to so much intense emotional involvement with another person, and I kept asking myself; what next? What happens when the holidays are over? I tried to stifle a yawn but Gilly noticed.

"It's okay, we can read the last letter some other time," she said but she looked disappointed and the last thing I wanted was to disappoint her, so I wrapped my arms around her and pulled her close.

"No way! You're not gonna leave me hanging! I'm not going home until I find out what happened to Norman. Did she find him? Is she bringing him back with her? Come on tell me."

Gilly shook her head. "I'll just read you her last letter. I've got it here."

Hi Darling,

It's hot in Mildura, I can see why they grow oranges here. A funny thing happened last night in the pub where I'm staying. It was just like in the pub up north a few months ago, an argument broke out at the bar where two men were having a drink. One man accused the other man of sleeping with his wife. They were both red in the face and dripping with sweat, both beer bellied and burping abuse at each other. They were burning with a rage that went deeper than jealousy. I thought that it wouldn't be long before they started communicating with their fists because neither of them seemed to understand the other's slurred words. I slipped into a corner booth and hid behind my shandy. Then one man yelled for the whole pub to hear, 'He's bottlin' his bloody spring water and sellin' it to the bloody pansies in the city while we die of thirst!' Then he shoved his fist in the other man's face and bellowed, 'Ya can keep me bloody wife mate, just give me some of ya bloody water!' Their angry voices just became a distant muffle after a while as I sat staring at a painting on the wall. It was that famous painting of the shearers, you know the one, by Tom Roberts. Remember, your dad took you to the art gallery to see it when you were a kid. All the people in the painting seem so happy, all working together like one big happy family, all doing an honest day's work for an honest day's pay. The main shearer at the front of the painting seems so capable, so good at his job. He grips the sheep with one strong arm and wields the blades with his other hand. The sheep doesn't struggle, it submits to the man's strength. There's not one nick on that sheep, not one drop of blood and the shearer's shirt is so clean. There's not one drop of sweat or oil, not one wrinkle on that pink shirt. While I was looking at it, I kept wondering why that shearer was wearing a pink shirt. I guessed that maybe it was his Sunday best and that maybe he was going out for dinner after work, and I could see that the colour was perfect for the painting but it still got on my nerves. It was as if that clean pink shirt was making fun of all the men who really work hard, men who sweat and get their hands dirty, their shirts dirty. It was as if that pink shirt was making fun of your dad. I used to love the way he'd come in at the end of the day, all streaked in dirt and sweat with his gumboots all mucky. Do you remember how he'd always give me a big hug and a kiss and I'd always push him away and tell him to take his dirty boots off. Then he'd go and have a good wash and we'd sit down to dinner. I'd look at his big strong hands holding his knife and fork and there'd always be a little rim of dirt under his finger nails. Your dad never owned a pink shirt. He always liked a crisp white shirt for his Sunday best. I miss him, I even miss his dirty footprints on the kitchen floor.

Anyway, the publican finally told the two men that were arguing, to settle their differences somewhere else and turfed them out. Later that night I asked the publican if he knew of anyone who might remember a boy passing through years ago, and he introduced me to one of his regulars, an old fella who'd been in the area his whole life. He said that years ago the police had come through making enquiries about a boy who'd gone missing. If anybody knew anything, they'd kept their mouths shut because there's a kind of boy that's got to make his own way in the world. It was nothing new.

I'm tired and I don't think I'll ever find Norman. I miss you and Nan. Why don't we meet in Ballarat and drive home together?

Love Mum.

"So, she never found him?" I asked. I felt disappointed. For some dumb reason I wanted a happy ending.

"No, but I think she found herself, or some way of being with herself without Dad."

Gilly's steady greyish green-eyed gaze threw me for a moment, and I couldn't help but think how amazing she was; the way she held it all together and didn't fall apart after all she'd been through. Although she sometimes seemed fragile, her feet were planted firmly on the ground and whatever forces of nature had fractured her family, growing up on a farm had made her wise.

Goodbyes

Two days after reading that last letter to me, Gilly and her nan packed up and left for Ballarat. People say; 'All roads lead to Rome,' and maybe they do in some parts of the world, but down here in the land of Oz it was becoming clear to me that all roads lead to Ballarat.

I remember Gilly's nan sitting at the wheel of her car, then winding down the window and telling Gilly to hurry up and hop in, it was time to get going. And I remember standing by the car and hugging Gilly before saying the dumbest thing I've ever said in my life; I said, "See ya next summer." I said it because that's what everybody always said at the end of summer. That's what Clancy and I always said. Me and Clancy never contacted each other during the year, we somehow didn't need to. We sort of knew how each other lived. The fact was, we lived separate lives, or maybe we just liked maintaining the mystery. Every summer we'd tell each other what had happened during the year. It didn't matter if things were exaggerated or not quite the truth. Anyway, truth has always been a bit slippery. We just liked believing each other. The fact was, Clancy was special and I kept him in a special compartment of my life, and maybe I just placed Gilly in that same special place. I smiled cheerfully at her and she gave me the strangest look, a little smile coated in pain. It was as if she expected me to say something else, but for some stupid reason it didn't occur to me to suggest that we see each other during the year. I don't know what made me think that 'the girl with the silver hair' would just magically appear again the next summer, as if life didn't happen between summers. She didn't say anything, she just got into the car and closed the door. Her nan turned on the ignition and they drove away.

I ambled back to our caravan, oblivious to whatever it was that Gilly was feeling. Mum was stretched out on her sun-lounge sipping tea and brooding. She was definitely down in the dumps and not in the mood for talking. Her eyes looked a bit red, like she'd been crying. I figured that Dad's departure had finally sunk in and she had begun to imagine what life would be like without him; life without someone to argue with. From the way she looked at me, I had a sneaking suspicion that I was about to become her next sparring partner, but all she said was that Zeke had come over to say goodbye. I had forgotten that the Zees were leaving.

Then just at that moment, out of the corner of my eye, a couple of flashes of pink zipped by, making their get-away, and hot on their heels was Ziggy chasing them and yelling for them to stop. I leapt onto the path and brought the twins to a halt. With Zelda under one arm and Zyana under the other, I told Ziggy to grab the tricycles, and I transported the girls back to camp Zee, where everyone was busy with the practicalities of packing up. Zeke's mum thanked me and chucked the girls into a couple of dirty washing baskets, then popped them into the mini-bus that she drove.

The site was lined with carefully labelled plastic tubs for shorts, T-shirts, towels, snorkels, sandals, board games and heaps of other stuff. Zeth and Zed were busily helping their dad lash a couple of canoes onto the roof of the four-wheel drive that Zachariah drove. He seemed so at ease, right in his element organizing everyone and calling out instructions.

Zeke was loosening off the guy ropes of the annex and taking out the pegs. When he saw me, he straightened up and gave me one of those big dazzling Zee smiles, then he said, "Guess who got the girl? I didn't see that coming!" He seemed genuinely pleased, like some great sportsman who'd lost a match to a worthy opponent. I just felt awkward; it wasn't exactly a competition from my perspective but he just kept grinning and nodding his head, so I hugged him and helped him to fold up the annex. Then I yelled to everyone, "See ya next summer!" and the whole gleaming crew lifted their heads and echoed, "See ya next summer!"

Half the park was clearing out that day and the whole place buzzed with car horns and goodbyes. It was one big crazy barn dance of caravans and four-wheel drives, side stepping each other as they trundled slowly along the narrow dirt paths to the exits, hoping that no one was coming in the opposite direction, forcing them to back-back their way out. There was no method to the madness and no one-way arrows to bring order to the chaos.

I knew Aaron's family would be shipping out, so I wandered over just as they were hooking their fishing boat onto their four-wheel drive. They always left their caravan on site for their grandparents' mini-season. Lachie, Bryce and Aaron barrelled up to me and Bryce yelled, "Race ya round the wreck!" So, in less than a heart-beat, we pelted into the water, laughing and splashing and dunking each other until it got too deep and we had to swim. Then round we went with the big paddle wheel towering over us, on a slight tilt. I wondered how long it would last before it joined its sister on the ocean floor. Bryce was a good swimmer, but not good enough to beat the big boys, so we let him win. When we got back it was time to go, so with hugs all round, we chanted, "See ya next summer!" and soon they were lost in the dust of the carnival of caravans.

The next day Clancy's family packed up and he came over to give Mum a hug goodbye.

"Have a good year. Be good. See ya next summer," said Mum cheerily."

"Yeah, see ya next summer," said Clancy. The cold wind whipping off shore wasn't half as cold as the glare he gave me. He was gonna make me shiver through the whole year.

The Milky Way

For some reason, with Gilly and Clancy gone, I felt more like myself and I wondered why being alone felt so comfortable. I felt unreasonably happy because I knew I had a few precious days alone to think and write, if only I could sidestep my mother and her relentless interest in everything I said or did.

I began to feel the old familiar tug of the city. It wasn't just the tantalizing sights, sounds and smells of cosmopolitan congestion that I craved, I couldn't wait to get back home to my computer and down the rabbit hole that I knew and loved. My instincts told me that on some subtle level, well under the radar of happy campers, the world had changed and that the players who pulled the strings were well on the way to designing more insidious acts of bastardry. I couldn't wait to toss around witticisms and world wary insights with my faceless, anonymous friends, some whose fanciful online identities I'd known since I was a kid playing online games. They were tireless researchers, citizen journalists or conspiracy theorists, dedicated to digging up the dirt, the hidden agendas of heinous hobgoblins. I missed the thrill of following the bread crumbs, the tenuous trail of information that always led to somewhere unexpected. We were online warriors, not persons of action, maybe only persons of interest, silent witnesses who joined the dots and passed on the connections through a netherworld of networks.

The night after Clancy left, I stood on the shore and stared up at the sky. The Milky Way arced all the way across the bay. I could see every star from Orion's Belt to the Pleiades and way over to the Southern Cross. The sky was a milky miasma of a million stars and galaxies, far, far away. I stood in silence, a solitary statue, and slowed my breath to an almost imperceptible halt. I was suspended in space, somewhere between this world and the next. I felt my heart thud slowly in its cage. It yearned to be free of me. Thud, thud; it drummed, its Neanderthal understanding of all that is.

An Unreliable Memoir

As I sit here finishing off this tale, this unreliable memoir, piecing together snippets of writing that I kept in an exercise book, hidden at the back of the board-games cupboard in the caravan; I guess I should explain that quite a few summers have passed since that summer; that special summer, when Gilly first came to the caravan park. And, I guess I should mention that the following summer, after not contacting her all year, she and Clancy turned up on New Years Eve holding hands. The rest of us were sitting around the fire having a drink, cracking jokes, and occasionally chucking a water bomb at someone's head for old time's sake, when I looked up and saw Gilly and Clancy walking towards us. It only took me a couple of seconds to figure out what must have happened during the year while I was off the radar, down some rabbit hole, determined to decipher the dynamics of the deep state; but for some reason I didn't feel jealous, I was just glad to see them. Clancy grinned and gave me one of his big bear hugs. Gilly just shrugged and got the giggles, which set-off Zara and Miranda. I deduced that the girls had probably been communicating all year.

As the night meandered towards midnight and we waited for the fireworks of Melbourne to explode, Clancy and Gilly told me their love story. Gilly had ended up moving to the centre of the universe, yeah Ballarat, to study psychology at the uni there and one night when she was out with friends at a pub, she bumped into Clancy. She said they just talked and talked, and as it turned out, they had more in common than I could ever have imagined. When I think of how much she loved that poem, 'Clancy of the Overflow,' I guess she was in love with Clancy long before she ever met him, and as she sat there with her head tilted up smiling at him, I don't think I'd ever seen 'the girl with the silver hair' quite so happy. As they were telling me their love story, I looked across the fire at Miranda laughing at something funny Shelton had said. She must have felt me looking at her because she turned her head and grinned, then stuck her middle finger up at me.

As for the present; well, some of us have completed university degrees or trade apprenticeships. Half the Zees are in high school and the other half are doing something connected to the environment. Zeke's a park ranger, Zara ended up studying environmental science and wants to work for Greenpeace, Zed's studying computer programming and runs his own website dedicated to environmental issues, Zeth bucked the trend and became a diesel mechanic working on big transport trucks. Zeb's about to start studying marine biology. I guess one of the Zees is going to 'heed the call' one day and end up a minister. Their mum didn't quite make the 'baker's dozen,' although she has had a couple more kids in the last five years, which brings the count to twelve, but she says she's stopping there. So Zeke has started spreading the rumour that there is an older half-brother up in Darwin somewhere.

My mate Aaron is a plumber and Bryce thinks he'll follow in his big brother's footsteps and start his apprenticeship when he finishes high school but who knows, he'll probably change his mind by then. Their brother Lachie had a few good professional fights and made a bit of money but decided to get out before his nose got broken, so he works as a trainer and is thinking of setting up his own mixed martial arts school. Hope is still as crazy about bugs as she was when she was eight and tells everyone that she wants to be an etymologist. And the Westies did a whole bunch of stuff.

As for Clancy's family; Jack became a chippy, he even got married and had a kid, which seems crazy because I feel like we're all still kids, but I guess he must have grown up because he's taken on the mantle of running the Fancy Dress Competition. Miranda just finished a degree in nursing, which is a bit strange because she never struck me as the compassionate type, but she really does have a great grin. And Clancy? Well, he always wanted to be a fireman but he became a sparky instead, which I guess is close enough.

Everyone seems to be doing something interesting or useful. As for me, I just finished my final year of a law degree. I did have a gap year, where I spent my time laying bricks until I knew I never wanted to lay another brick in my life. I guess the cure for laying bricks is laying bricks! But the truth is, when I watched my boss work, I was in awe of the mathematical skill and precision he brought to bear as he created mandala-like patterns in the paving of people's courtyards. Then once, when I was washing down his artistry with a high-pressure hose, I turned and knocked him off his feet and as he lay there sopping wet and semi-conscious, I decided that I was too mathematically challenged and way too clumsy to be a brickie. So, I decided to try and elevate my self-esteem by becoming a lawyer, but all studying law has taught me is that I don't want to be a lawyer. So I guess I'm back where I started, that summer, at the end of high school, when I didn't have a clue who I was, or where I was going or what I wanted to be, and my head swirled with a million possibilities, but I don't think any of us are defined by what we do for a living. What strikes me most about my Indented friends is their generosity of spirit and the fact that we all just accept each other for who we are. Back in Melbourne whenever anyone asks me, "What are you doing for New Years Eve?" I always say, "I know exactly where I'll be on New Years Eve."

As I look across to the other side of the bay, over towards Frankston, Rosebud and Sorrento; for the first time since I started coming here, I don't feel like there's someone on the other side gazing back. Most of the caravan parks on the other side closed this summer because of some strange mutant virus that scientists say they don't know much about. So I'm glad to be here in the parallel universe of Indented Head, where the virus seems far, far away. There are rumours that people are dying on the other side of the bay; the virus takes their breath away. I've heard that death doesn't take long, just a day or two and that the lucky few who survive are never quite the same. There's talk of a vaccine, an experiment developed 'at the speed of science;' funny because I always thought science moved slowly. Maybe the virus will run its course before it crosses the bay. Also, there's a lock down in the city to try and stop the spread. No one within a twenty-kilometre radius can get out and no one outside of the lockdown zone can get in, so I guess we'll be staying down here for a while …. And if anything bad did happen, this is the place I'd choose to be and these are the people I'd choose to be with.

As I lift my head, I see Mum and Dad stretched out on their sun-lounges staring out to sea and I can't help wondering which one of us has the most 'indented' head; all three of us seem a bit crazy. Dad still comes down for a while at the beginning of the season to help set up and have a bit of a holiday. He's probably daydreaming about the time he sailed across the Bay of Bengal and Mum is probably lost in some snow storm in New York City.

She must have felt me gazing at her because she looks up and gives me one of her best smiles, then for no reason, no reason at all, she draws an infinity sign in mid-air. I bend down and pick up a handful of sand and as it falls between my fingers, I'm reminded of the words of that poem; 'To see a world in a grain sand …'.

Author's note and acknowledgements

This book is a work of fiction. However, some characters and events were inspired by real people and real events.

Thanks to those fellow campers at Indented Head who encouraged me to write the novel, and in particular I would like to thank the kids. It was a pleasure to watch you grow. Finally, thank you to Gabriel for some nice editorial advice.

I would like acknowledge that the verse quoted from the poem 'Clancy of the Overflow' was written by Banjo Paterson.